WARREN FRIEND curr
originally from a small villag

Warren has worked in
his life. *Moon Henge* is his d
him well will find it hard to believe. warren love
and the mystical world.

MOON HENGE

WARREN FRIEND

SilverWood

Published in 2023 by SilverWood Books

SilverWood Books Ltd
14 Small Street, Bristol, BS1 1DE, United Kingdom
www.silverwoodbooks.co.uk

ISBN 978-1-80042-225-4 (paperback)

British Library Cataloguing in Publication Data
A CIP catalogue record for this book is
available from the British Library

Page design and typesetting by SilverWood Books

This book contains realistic action and fight scenes that some parents/carers might like to review before passing this book to their child.

CHAPTER ONE

Molly became aware that she was awake just before her head hit the hard metal exterior of her home. An old, veiny, but still incredibly strong hand was swinging her by the hair and had just let go. The metal was unforgiving and Molly's head was still ringing as Mank, her cat, followed in her path and was now sitting on her head. Unfortunately, Mank was a little unkempt and his nails were long. Blood trickled down the side of Molly's face and the stinging added to her headache.

These attacks had recently become more frequent. The palace guards were getting increasingly agitated and desperate to satisfy the king. Molly knew something big was happening, for it was the king's own guard and they were currently in Molly's home and in the Fogey's neighbourhood, in the roughest part of town and on one of the roughest places on the Moon.

Yes, that's right. Molly lived on the Moon and her home, for want of a better word, was a ramshackle dwelling made from a shiny, hard metal that Molly had found while out foraging for food. Molly called her house Sate because she thought it sounded cute and homely. However, in reality, Sate was the wording printed on one of the house panels. Some of the letters were missing and when completed, it spelled the word 'satellite'. It was, in fact, an object from a different world that, unbeknown to Molly, fate was guiding her towards.

Mank – shortened from Manky – was so called because he and Molly made each other's acquaintance one day as the butcher kicked the cat out of his shop, swearing, "Get that manky cat out of my shop," although, in truth, his language was much stronger.

Molly saved the cat from being killed and they quickly became best friends. Mank was a flea-bitten and very scruffy creature, with one ear pointed straight up and the other, a half-ear with bite marks, flopped over. Most of Mank's teeth were missing, although one protruded slightly outside his mouth, giving him a slightly weird look. Mostly, he relied on Molly for food; he loved her very much.

As Molly reached for the small rock beside her on the ground, determined to catch the guard right between the eyes, her only other friend, Pod, stood on her hand. A small yelp of pain escaped Molly's lips and she dropped the rock.

"What did you do that for?" she mouthed at Pod.

"Don't be a stupid idiot all your life," Pod replied. "They will chop your hands off for that."

Molly wasn't sure that Pod was really a friend but she guessed it was as close as you could get. He only seemed to enjoy her company when he was tormenting her or pulling her hair. But she knew he enjoyed her hunting skills as, more often than not, that was what kept them alive.

Molly was an orphan. She had never known her parents and had lived on the streets all her life. Her knowledge of the streets and their hidden passages had saved her life on more than one occasion and it was down one of these narrow passages that Pod now dragged her. The guards were emptying her prized possessions out onto the street. It didn't look like there was much of value, but Molly knew different – those few items represented her life. She was angry and was determined to discover what exactly was happening. The guards, bored by now, were already moving on to the next part of town.

CHAPTER TWO

Molly returned to her pile of belongings and began to put them back in their set places. This was Molly's life – her hunting pack, the finest twine rope, which was her most valuable possession, said to be spun from the finest moon dust and Glorb beams. It was fine and strong and was rumoured to hold magic properties. Molly had awoken one morning to find it wrapped in loose paper with a note attached. She still had the note and read it most nights, even though she now knew the words by heart.

She withdrew the note from her hidden pocket and read the words again. They brought her a mixture of comfort, sadness and joy. She had no idea who the letter was from but she could tell that the paper it was written on was expensive and of the finest quality. In the ten years since she had received the note, it had never torn or faded.

The note said, "Happy Birthday Molly. I wish I could offer you a secure future. You are very important but I am afraid it is far too dangerous for you at the moment. Please look after this rope and it will look after you. It was made by the mystical moon miners thousands of years ago and has great properties. Take care Molly and I will look out for you when I can."

Molly often pondered those words and fell asleep with them ringing in her head. She had asked about and discovered that the moon miners were an ancient tribe that lived underground in the craters. They mined the raw precious metals that were in abundance on the Moon. They were excellent climbers and acrobats, often climbing straight down into craters and engaging in very dangerous work. The miners and their goods were highly valued and their equipment was always of the highest quality. The Rord, as it was known, was neither rope nor cord, and its name was associated with the finest of the fine. It was the stuff of legend, and now it was Molly's. Had the guard recognised the Rord it would now be around his waist and no longer Molly's. Luckily for her, the guard dismissed her belongings as an undesirable something he had had the misfortune of stepping in.

The next year, on her birthday, Molly received a knife wrapped in the same paper. Like the Rord, the knife was made of the finest quality and was bejewelled with stones that Molly guessed came from the moon miners. It was as sharp as a moon slither fish's tooth which, if you don't know, is very very sharp. Molly kept it hidden in her oldest smelliest boot. This kept prying eyes away and if any curious hand happened to reach inside the smelly boot, it would quickly lose some fingers. Molly had created an ingenious hiding place so that the knife could only be retrieved by way of a secret compartment in the heel. As a result, the guard and the many thieves and pickpockets that roamed around remained unaware of Molly's truly valuable items. They had come close to discovery on several occasions. The worst was when the notorious bully, Griffer, had fancied the boot for himself. After losing three of his toes and eventually his foot to the onset of moon rot, he was now known as Griffer One Foot. He was still a terrible bully, but he left Molly well alone, believing her to be a witch who had cursed his foot and made it fall off.

Unfortunately, the knife, though clearly very valuable, had arrived unaccompanied by a note. Unbeknown to Molly, in certain secret circles, the knife was revered and had been known by many different names throughout history. The most popular of these names was the Nitsplitter, so called because not only could it split hairs, it could split the nits that lived on the hair.

Molly had collected other bits and pieces over the years – shiny moon crystals and a rather useful set of skeleton keys that she had stolen from a drunken bumster outside the moozer, which was a particularly famous moonshine house frequented by both thieves and bandits and by the rich, gullible and noteworthy. When she was hungry or looking for things to pilfer, Molly often went there because she knew the pickings were rich. She would then exchange the loot for food in the foggy underworld. Sometimes, certain items took her fancy. The set of skeleton keys was one such item. Molly didn't know that the previous owner of the keys was a notorious villain, Scarro, who had his suspicions, but couldn't prove that Molly was the culprit.

CHAPTER THREE

Right now, his Moon Monkeys were watching Molly collect her possessions. The Moon Monkeys were particularly vicious creatures with very large feet. This was very good for balance and power on the Moon, although one of their more unsavoury characteristics was the ability to flatten someone's head by stamping on it very quickly. This was a feat that the leader of this particular vicious group, Chunky, was hoping to perform on Molly as soon as possible.

Molly suddenly noticed that Pod had vanished. This was not a good sign. She also noticed that Mank's moth-eaten half-tail was twitching like a moon bean on a lava plate – another sure sign of danger. "Thanks," Molly uttered to Mank, as she quickly gathered her belongings and rolled swiftly sideways.

Seconds later, the big foot of Chunky the Moon Monkey landed exactly where Molly had been. The power of the stamp forced Chunky to lose balance, allowing Molly to make her escape.

"Get her," shouted Chunky to his gang.

Molly sprinted down the small alleys of the Fogey's.

The Moon Monkeys were very quick and Molly ran for her life. Her heart was bursting through her chest, she pumped her legs and arms as hard as she could, but the Moon Monkeys were gaining ground and Molly was struggling. Suddenly, Mank dived from a moon rock straight onto the lead Monkey's face. The cat's nails raked down the Monkey's face, causing him to slow and then stumble. The second Monkey ploughed straight into the back of the first and both tumbled to the ground. By now, however, Chunky had dusted himself down and was in hot pursuit. Mank's actions had gained Molly some valuable time so she used it wisely. As she rounded a corner in the alley, she spotted a hole in the wall. Heading for this hole, she dived through the gap. Once through, she grabbed a nearby bush and forced it into the hole to cover her tracks. As she forced the bush into the gap the plant gave off a most amazing smell. It was like nothing Molly had ever smelled before. If she had known of such a thing, Molly would have recognised the smell as a mix of incense, jasmine and diamonds.

Yes, on the Moon, diamonds have a lush, rich, pleasant smell.

The intoxicating smell made Molly feel dizzy and she stumbled back. When she looked up, she found herself in a lush, green garden. The sights were amazing, with plants of every colour of the rainbow. Molly had never seen such sights and they took her breath away. There was grass, which was something that Molly had never seen before. It felt amazing as it tickled her toes poking out through the holes in her shoes. A river ran into a small pond where strange bird-like creatures rested on the water. These unbelievable sights caused a sweet sensual overload.

Suddenly, Molly had to duck as an amazing flutterby flew towards her. Molly had only heard about such creatures in the nursery rhymes overheard near the school gates. Molly liked to hide near the school and gained much of her knowledge that way. It was strange then, that she now found herself here with a flutterby inches from her face. The nursery rhymes were right; they were truly awesome. She lifted her hand and the strange creature landed on her finger and began to vibrate, showering Molly's hand with gold dust. As the vibrations sped up a strange humming sound came from the creature's wings, not unlike the purring of a cat.

Molly felt light-headed and dizzy. The humming and purring increased to a magnificent crescendo, and suddenly she had a dreamlike vision. She saw elegant ladies with perfect hair and make-up and complexions as pale as the landscape around them, dressed in the finest moon fabrics. This was considered the height of fashion among the aristocracy and the wealthy.

The vision continued and expanded, the walls were adorned with the finest tapestries and a huge ornate chandelier hung in the centre of the room, glistening in the bright light that shone through the huge windows, scattering tiny light crystals around the room. Three of the ladies were peering into an elaborately decorated cot, covered in gems and crystals. There, in the cot, wrapped in the finest fabrics, lay a beautiful baby girl. Out of the blue, Molly was spiralling back into her own body and the vision disappeared in a flash. She was back in the garden. The flutterby on her hand was glowing but it began to shake rapidly and the colours began to flash. Molly recognised this as a warning. In an instant, the flutterby disappeared. Molly had little time to comprehend the meaning of these strange events. She could hear voices getting louder as they came closer. She quickly ducked behind a beautifully coloured and luxurious bush.

Two men approached. Molly instantly recognised the king and, although not as familiar to her, she knew the other man to be General Clutterberry, general of the king's entire moon army. The pair stopped just close enough for Molly to hear their words. The king was agitated.

"We must be ready," he shouted at the general. "I want and need this revenge. I demand it. Victory will be mine."

General Clutterberry looked pale and nervous. "Patience, Sire, please. Everything must be in place before we proceed."

The king stomped his feet and glared at the general. "Enough excuses. This must happen and soon. I have waited years for this!"

With this strange sentence ringing out, the king turned heel and stormed off. The general was left to chase after the king, trying to placate him all the way.

Molly could tell this was important. The king was known for his temper and lack of patience, and the general looked very worried. Molly was concerned. It was time to get out of this place and go have a word with Pod. She climbed back through the hole in the wall and returned home without further incident. Mank was waiting for her return. She scooped Mank into her arms, collapsed on her bed and promptly fell asleep, although her dreams were fitful.

CHAPTER FOUR

Molly was awoken by a very unpleasant smell. "Oh Mank, you stink," she said, throwing the cat out of the door. Once she had cleared the fog of her sleep and the room, she began to recall the strange events of the day before. She was relieved that the Moon Monkeys hadn't found her. They were not the brightest. They still hadn't figured out where she lived.

Molly felt that she needed to talk and the only person she could talk to was Pod. Mank, although a good listener, was never very good at replying, although he seemed to purr at the correct moments. Molly set off to find Pod, knowing that he could be anywhere. She didn't know where Pod lived; he just appeared when he wanted something.

Pod had his own secrets. He was, at that moment, bent over a chair being thrashed to within an inch of his life. Another lash of the belt rained down on Pod's small frame. The pain was excruciating but Pod was determined to keep his mouth shut. He would not give his dad's wife, Angel, the satisfaction. She was as far from an angel as Pod thought possible. He could not bring himself to call her Mum because, technically, she wasn't. Pod's father had had a mistress, who was Pod's real mum.

Unfortunately, Pod did not know his true mother, as she had dumped him at the gates of his father's house and disappeared. Angel had hated and despised Pod ever since. Pod's father, as a governor, held a relatively high position in government and, as such, was frightened of the shame that Pod could bring to him and his family. Although Pod's father was powerful in the realm, Angel ruled the roost, and he was secretly scared of this mad woman. Although Angel wanted Pod dead, and it would have made the governor's life a whole lot easier, his father could never quite bring himself to kill the young Pod. Therefore, he came to a compromise which was of little benefit to Pod. He abandoned Pod in the moon slums to fend for himself. Pod, however, was required to occasionally present himself at the family home to alleviate his father's guilt. Although his father, in his own way, cared deeply for his son, he was more scared of Angel's wrath. When possible, he gave Pod what little money or food he managed to conceal from Angel to ensure that his son survived.

Pod would have stopped visiting long ago and could have spent his life without his father and his father's wife. He couldn't have cared less about them. But two things in that household were very important to him – his younger twin brother and sister, Oodle and Poodle. They both adored their older brother. Pod bathed in the looks of devotion and unabashed love that radiated from their tiny faces every time they saw him. He would gladly die for them and it was this that drew him back to the house time after time. He wanted to make sure that they were safe and secure, although, to be fair, Angel seemed to dote on them and see to their every need. However, Pod knew (and was currently experiencing) what could happen if you made Angel mad. He vowed to kill her if she ever laid a finger on the darling beautiful twins.

The current beating was because of the three doogle coins, about enough for a loaf of two-day-old bread, that Pod's father had sneaked to him. His father had hoped that Angel had not seen him do it, but she seemed to have a sixth sense about these things. The governor stood by the kitchen sink washing up and staring at Pod. It was his father's inaction and silence that finally made Pod cry.

"Enough," his father shouted suddenly.

This shocked the room, which was engulfed in silence. Angel let go of Pod and, with a sly cuff to the ear, told him in no uncertain terms to clear off. The boy took this opportunity to scarper, leaving his father to face Angel's anger.

Pod knew he should feel sorry for his father but couldn't quite bring himself to admit such an emotion. Instead, he left the door clanging in the dust of his speedy escape.

CHAPTER FIVE

Pod had only one thing on his mind – to find Molly, Mank and the relative safety of the Sate. Although the Sate was ramshackle, Pod thought of it as a safe haven where he could be himself and belong. He charged away from his father's house, which he never thought of as his home. He raced further through the town until he reached the outskirts of the Fogey's. The pain gradually began to subside. He had more pain in his heart than in his actual butt cheeks. He screeched around the corner and smacked straight into the onrushing Molly. The crash threw them both into the air and they promptly landed on their rears. Given recent events, this was much more painful for Pod.

"Where in the moon pit have you been?" shouted Molly. The moon pit was a place very similar to Hell.

"Hello to you, Molly," screeched Pod. "Nice to see you!"

Molly was a little upset and, although she was used to Pod's certain attitude, this was curt even for him. "I was worried and have been searching for you," she cried. "Where have you been?"

"Nothing to do with you and I don't want to talk about it," Pod retorted.

Molly had known Pod for some time and she could tell that he was serious. He pulled a scowl when he was angry, with deep lines crossing his still young face, making him look world-weary. Molly knew better than to try to coax answers from him and wisely decided not to push matters. However, she had decided that she had to get to the bottom of Pod's secrets. Every time he disappeared, he returned in this foul mood, and recently those moods had been getting worse.

Molly knew one sure way to improve Pod's mood and that was through his stomach. He looked like he hadn't eaten in days and Molly knew that moonster bat was his favourite.

"Right," said Molly, giving Pod a playful prod in the ribs, "I feel as if I haven't eaten for days. Time for some serious food." She really hadn't eaten for days and her last meal had been stolen from rats enjoying some after-moozer leftovers. They were most disgruntled when Molly disturbed their free tea and stole the leftover pie. Although cold and half nibbled by rats, the crocopig pie had been delicious. But her stomach was now telling her that this was a distant memory.

If they could, the pair would feast on moonsters all day and night. Unfortunately, they were very difficult to catch, and required a half-day trip across desolate and hazardous terrain.

"C'mon," said Molly. "If we start now, we will be there for dusk."

Dusk was the prime time to hunt the bats, as they left their crater dwellings to feast on the moon insects that flew across the crater swamps at night.

Although Pod wasn't feeling at all happy, he knew that Molly was right. His stomach grumbled and he imagined a nice juicy moonster bat roasted over a warm camp fire. Molly set off with a purpose about her stride, looking confident but secretly hoping that Pod would follow.

"Hey up," he called after her. "Wait for me. You need someone to help you eat them!" Pod had only ever managed to catch one bat and that had more to do with luck than judgement. He could only watch in awe at the magic of Molly's undoubted skill at catching these elusive creatures.

The terrain was rough and unforgiving and they had to stop a few times to take on water and nibble on some weeds and scrubs they found along the way. They needed to keep their strength up as it would be required very soon. Up hillocks, down through small craters while dodging the larger ones, they gradually made progress. This area of the Moon was very desolate and the pair were tiring.

Suddenly, Molly stopped. Her nose had started to twitch and the smell was rather unpleasant. The bats' feeding ground and home were located close to the sulphur swamps. The area was pungent, to say the least. No one wanted to visit this area and those who did never stayed long. Indeed, if a particularly bad sulphur cloud drifted your way, the chances of surviving it were very slim indeed. Many a hunter had ventured into the swamps never to be seen again. There were rumours and legends of mysterious monsters that lived in these clouds. Molly had never seen any such creatures and, as she had never heard of anyone surviving the clouds, the stories couldn't be proven. She did, however, believe that if it wasn't for the succulent bat meat then everyone would give this entire region a very wide berth.

Pod, now with a peg over his nose, pointed to a nearby crater. The first of the evening bats were soaring out of the dark depths and high up into the night sky. The pair set about creeping towards the large dark crater. Dodging behind boulders, they approached the edge of the dark cavernous pit. Once at the edge, they paused to collect their wits and prepare. Catching a moonster required great skill and courage. Only a skilled hunter could catch one of these beasts and few even tried. Molly was one of the best and, even though she rarely thought well of herself, she knew that she wasn't half bad.

Pod thought Molly was awesome and possibly the best bat hunter on the entire Moon. He had heard rumours of the legendary hunter Carnaverous the Great who would return with sacks of bats. Pod was convinced that Molly was even better.

Molly unwound the Rord, tied an old-school cowboy lasso and began to spin it above her head. Faster and faster the slick coil spun until Pod could no longer see the Rord. He could still sense that it was there from the slight high-pitched hum it made as it cut through the thin moon atmosphere at incredible speed.

All of a sudden, Molly flicked her wrist and the Rord flew from her hand with the velocity and intensity of a bullet.

Across the crater it flew, encircling a slim tower of rock that Pod couldn't even see.

Molly now pulled the Rord hard across the chasm, making it taut, and then quickly tied it around a rocky outcrop on her side of the crater to create a tightrope. Next, she removed her tired, worn and holey shoes and asked Pod if he was ready. Pod, nervous and in awe of the slim athletic Molly, could only nod in reply.

Barefoot, Molly sprung onto the tight Rord, wobbled a little until she found her balance and then gave Pod the thumbs up as she slowly but surely began to make her way towards the centre of the crater. Her slim feet seemed to curl around the Rord, as she felt the magic cords with her sensitive toes. She could feel herself becoming one with the Rord. She felt the slight breeze vibrating against the tightly spun strings and, if she concentrated, she could hear magical musical notes emanating from the delicate Rord. The music was melodic and haunting, the sound otherworldly; no moon musicians could play chords so sweet or delicate.

The sound played on Molly's ear, relaxed her and prepared her. It was as if the Rord knew Molly and was gently encouraging her to progress. Once at the centre, Molly gradually calmed her senses and waited, patiently and gracefully balanced on the Rord. She began breathing more slowly and deeply, relaxing her muscles, clearing her mind and focusing on the task at hand. Like a statue, Molly waited, silent and perfectly poised, her senses honed.

Quickly and without warning, a moonster bat flew past Molly's taut body. She let it pass. Another dozen or so bats

25

flew out and she let them pass too, their breath and odour close enough to make an inexperienced hunter flinch. But Molly remained motionless, patiently waiting.

Suddenly, with reflexes quicker than a cat, Molly extended her arm, flicked her wrist and caught the nearest unfortunate bat by the neck. With lightning speed, her other hand moved and, before the bat could sink its powerful fangs into her arm, she sliced the bat's head completely off with the Nitsplitter. Green blood spurted from the creature. Molly ignored the slight burning sensation from the blood on her skin and threw the still warm body into a sack tied around her waist. One, two, three more bats swiftly followed the first one. With two each, Molly now had enough, as she never believed in taking more than was required.

"One more," shouted Pod on seeing Molly prepare to return along the tightrope. "One more. We need one for Mank," he shouted.

Although Mank was nowhere to be seen, Molly knew her loyal pal would not be far away. "Okay," she said as she repositioned herself for the next catch.

Suddenly, a swarm of about twenty bats surged up out of the darkness. Squeaking and squawking, the lead bats crashed into Molly, knocking her off balance. The smell of the creatures in such numbers was nauseating. Some were in her face scratching to escape, their claws pulling at her hair. Molly knew she was in trouble! The Rord began to swing and she could feel her weight shift. She knew that if she didn't react swiftly, she would be plunged into the deep dark abyss and certain death.

Abruptly, she squatted down on her haunches. With skill and grace, she sprang up into the air. The Rord was left swinging below her, as she flipped in the air and performed a back somersault. Even the great acrobats of the moon circus would have been proud. Molly's head passed her feet in a feat of amazing agility. Momentarily, she was facing down into the crater before she quickly righted herself. The lead foot missed the Rord but, luckily, the trailing foot gripped it and her toes wrapped around the quivering coil.

The moment hung in the balance. Molly teetered. The next few seconds were critical. She teetered first one way and then the other. It seemed she would surely lose her grip and plunge to her doom. But almost imperceptibly, the swinging Rord began to slow. As Molly swung less violently, she began to gain control.

"Come on, Molly!" shouted Pod. "You can make it."

As Molly regained her balance she carefully hurried to the crater's edge. Back on firm ground, she lay on her back and laughed, the adrenaline slowly draining from her. Unbelievably, one of the bats was still flapping and pulling on her hair. Pod had to help the stricken Molly and the panicked bat to disentangle. After a while, the patient Molly and the somewhat less patient bat were free of each other.

"Look," said Molly, "it's only a baby." The bat was tiny. It hopped around on the dust attempting to fly.

"It can't even fly," said Pod. "Let's kill it."

"It must have fallen from its mother's clasp in the confusion," Molly replied. "I have already ruined the poor creature's life. I will not kill it. I will nurse the baby until it can fend for itself."

Pod grumbled and groaned, but Molly was adamant.

"Fine," he said. "But it looks like a rat." And, thus, the baby bat acquired its name and from that day on was known as Ratabat. Molly scooped Ratabat up and tucked it into her breast pocket.

CHAPTER SIX

"Let's escape this foul-smelling place, light a fire and cook our bounty," said Pod.

"Watching you work has made me hungry." Molly threw a playful kick at Pod and set off at a brisk trot. "Come on, then," she chuckled over her shoulder.

It wasn't long before Pod and Molly were sitting by a roaring fire. Ratabat could feel the warmth from the fire and wriggled in Molly's pocket. Molly lifted the small creature out of her pocket and set it onto the ground. She wasn't sure if it was male or female, so, for the time being, Ratabat was an 'it'.

Ratabat didn't care as it crawled about on the ground, trying its hardest to stand and then, with little hops, to fly. Unfortunately, it wasn't having much success and kept falling face first into the dust. Suddenly, Mank pounced on the little bat, threw it up in the air and was about to swallow it whole.

"No," screamed Molly, as she launched herself into a dive and caught Ratabat, rolled through the dirt and righted herself.

"Bad Mank. Ratabat is the newest member of our little team," she scolded the cat. Mank looked somewhat sheepish and none too impressed with this turn of events. Worse was to come as Molly gave Mank a swift kick. "Now, time to make friends. Please go and catch Ratabat some swamp insects for tea. If you behave and come back with some food, we may let you share in the moonster feast."

Mank sloped off with his manky tail between his legs, although the thought of the succulent freshly cooked meat to come soon cheered him up. He wasted no time in returning with his mouth full of big juicy swamp insects. He dropped them in front of Ratabat, who began to do a weird little wobbly jig. Obviously overjoyed with this offering, Ratabat staggered to Mank and gave him a bat-like kiss. The cat blew the baby bat back, causing it to tumble over. Mank then turned tail but secretly accepted the weird little creature. Ratabat righted itself and started to tuck into the tasty morsels – tasty if you were a baby bat that is. Soon, with a belly full of insects, Ratabat lay snoring softly in front of the fire. Molly, aware that eating the poor bat's friends and family might not be a good idea in front of it, had been waiting for this moment to begin cooking her catch. Within the hour, the entire intrepid gang were asleep in front of the warming fire. The flames flicked and danced across their still faces and for the first time, all four slept soundly and with their bellies full.

CHAPTER SEVEN

Meanwhile, sitting in front of his own roaring fire, King Rufus stared through an ornately decorated telescope. He was looking at the patterned planet that appeared bright and illuminated through his eyepiece.

As he stared, his eyes glazed over and his mind wandered back to the terrifying time that has sculptured his whole life so far. Rufus was a prince at the time and only young, but the events were burned into his memory. It had been a time of prosperity and happiness on the Moon. For generations, the young prince's parents had ruled kindly and well. After many turbulent years, the Moon was enjoying stability and normality, so the strange events that unfolded were unheard of. The invading alarms rang for two days – a shrilling high-pitched noise that was absorbed by everything and everyone. People were frightened and jittery; no one really knew what was going on. The army was raised to a state of emergency not seen since the Great War. The Wise Ones and moon scientists stared endlessly at the sky with their strange instruments. The king took the unprecedented decision to evacuate the city and the surrounding outlying villages.

For days, the people moved their possessions, carrying all that they possible could, with wagons and carts loaded until the wheels bent and then a little more added for good measure. This was a huge disruption that tore up the fabric of normality and civilisation. The citizens headed for the large craters in the Byzantine crater sea. This large dry area was composed of huge craters and was the perfect place to hide large numbers of people. Despite protests and advice from his politicians and senior advisors, the old king refused to follow his loyal subjects. He was resolute in his belief that the correct place for a king and his family was at their ancestral home.

The alarms stopped almost as abruptly as they had started. Even the young Rufus could sense the nervous expectation in the air. The towns and villages were deserted. The castle was an eerie ghost-like place, and the few who remained were holed up in the great hall with the doors barricaded and heavily guarded. Rufus was at his father's side, listening intently to the hushed discussions.

"I do believe that we will be in luck, Sire," the Chief of Science excitedly told the king. "My projections and belief are that the strange object approaching will land in the wildernesses of the Seven Moonscape Wastelands of Raja."

"Well, we need to track it," said the king. "I need to know what is happening. Bring the elite king's guard and my family."

"Sire, is it not too dangerous to take the young prince and your wife?" pleaded the Chief of the Guard.

"No, we haven't the time or men to spare. We have no choice. They must come!"

It was with these words that the reluctant Prince Rufus was placed upon a moomal, a camel-like creature, and shortly afterwards set off with a small but elite company towards the wastelands. As they were travelling, they could see with the naked eye the large bright burning shape in the sky. It was rather like the mysterious comets that sometimes streaked over the sky, only larger and brighter. However, rather than racing at the speed of light across the sky, this object appeared to be slowing and getting closer and larger. The group made the wastelands and the well-camouflaged camp in record time.

The old king had taken the wise decision to watch and wait, and see what unfolded; only fools rush in. Never one to make a rash decision, the king's steadiness on this occasion probably saved all their lives. The approaching object was very close now. It began to blot out the stars and patterned planet behind it. From this hiding place, the small Rufus watched the events take shape. The glowing ball of intense light and heat slowed and then stopped, before hovering some way above their heads.

Like a child watching a particularly scary film, Rufus peeked at the spectacle from behind his father's cloak and between his fingers that he held over his face. Smoke and steam bellowed from what was now clearly some form of strange craft. The moon folk had never seen anything like it before. Flames suddenly shot from the bottom, the noise increased and Rufus had to take his hands away from his eyes to cover his ears. Four long tentacle-type rods appeared out of the smoke, gradually stretching and folding down. To Rufus, they looked very similar to the deadly tarrantlunlar spider, only much larger and more mechanical.

The craft now drifted down to the surface of their home. The roar was deafening, and dust and small rocks were thrown into the air. The king's party shrank further into their hiding places. The flames began to die down as the craft approached the surface. Without warning, a huge sheet shot from the top of the craft, with thin ropes attaching the sheet to the strange craft. The sheet suddenly billowed and expanded, causing the falling craft to rapidly slow its descent.

The fire burners slowly decreased until there was only a soft glow before they disappeared completely. Soon, the smoke and dust began to settle too. Rufus now had a clearer picture of the unwelcome stranger intent on entering his homeland. The giant spider-like craft landed on the surface of the young prince's home with a soft thud, the metal legs supporting the main body of the craft. About the size of two large carts, like the ones often seen at the moon markets, the craft was very shiny and it shimmered in the translucent moonlight.

Suddenly there was a loud whooshing noise and a section of the metal was pushed outwards. A doorway began to appear in the side of the strange object. Rufus shook with fear and could feel nervous, worried tension emanating in waves from the assembled group. Despite being fearless fighters, the king's party were obviously frightened and prepared for the worst. There was a subtle soft glow from inside the craft and a ladder dropped from the door to the moon surface. The watching soldiers, preparing to charge the intruder, became impatient with their own inactivity and were overtaken with battle lust.

"No," shouted the king. "We must watch and wait." Again, the king in his wisdom knew not to rush in against the unexplained.

Incredibly, it appeared to young Rufus as if a huge pair of feet were searching for a grip on the first rung of the ladder. When thick white legs began to appear from the doorway, Rufus knew he was right – they were huge feet. A white ghost-like figure, with huge cylindrical tanks attached to its back, began to descend the ladder backwards towards the surface of the king's land.

Once on the surface, the intruder turned towards the watching party. Rufus dropped his jaw in shock – the creature had no face, but merely a huge oval black eye; an eye that never blinked but simply stared at Rufus, making the prince want to run away as fast as he possibly could. Completely white and with big heavy boots, the creature suddenly leapt in the air and covered a vast distance in one giant step. The king's party were ready to turn and flee, but the king held his arm aloft and the years of power and respect he had garnered held the group in check. The stranger began to extend a long pole that was sharply pointed at one end. To Rufus it looked like a particularly vicious weapon, but the figure merely jammed it hard into the moon surface.

Another beast joined the first, making the assembled

watchers even more nervous. How many of them were there in the craft? The second one carried a piece of rectangular material with red, white and blue stripes and little star-like shapes. The second alien attached the material to the pole, and then both stood very still and raised their thick white arms up to their one eye.

Rufus didn't know what was happening, but it looked serious and almost like the soldiers' ceremonies back at the castle.

CHAPTER EIGHT

Once they had completed this ritual, the creatures began to dig around on the surface. They filled little jars with soil and picked up small pieces of rock. Rufus thought this was most strange and wondered why they wanted old moon rock. For what seemed like hours, the two strange creatures prodded and probed and leapt about. They had a small machine that they seemed to delightedly press every so often, causing the machine to emit a bright flash that blinded Rufus for seconds at a time. Although most strange, this machine appeared to cause no lasting damage and Rufus soon stopped feeling frightened of it.

After some time, a third creature appeared at the entrance to the craft. This made the armed guards clutch their weapons even tighter and gnash their teeth. They wanted and were prepared to attack. Fed up with inactivity and the need to avenge this intrusion, they were tensed like coiled springs, ready to explode into action. The third creature, however, didn't descend the steps. It merely beckoned to its colleagues. The two already on the ground acknowledged the third and, after a flurry of activity, and more seemingly never-ending flashes, they gradually began to move back to the strange craft.

Relief surged through the onlookers as they realised that the aliens were preparing to leave. The palpable tension began to evaporate and, although they would remain professional until the craft had departed, there was a softening in the bodies of the armed soldiers. The taut fingers that hovered over the weapons, ready to thrust, pull, push and cut, began to relax. The second creature, now back at the steps, began to slowly climb into the craft. Finally, this white beast, that had had the nerve to land on the Moon, approached the craft. It stopped abruptly, turned and looked directly at Rufus and the king's men. Rufus felt the unblinking black-eyed stare directly on him, boring into his soul.

The creature began to take a step towards the group. Rufus held his breath. Surely, the creature could not know that they were there. Rufus believed that they were well camouflaged and well hidden from sight, but it appeared that the intruder knew they were there but was completely unable to see them; only a sixth sense from the creature seemed to feel their presence. More than one step and the game would be up. Battle and bloodshed would ensue, Rufus was sure of it.

Suddenly, the creature at the top of the steps began to wave and shout, grabbing the attention of the beast which turned to look at the craft. The creature at the top of the steps pointed to his wrist. Reluctantly, the last intruder moved back towards the craft. Rufus, who had been holding his breath the whole time, let out a huge sigh of relief. The creatures were definitely leaving and a nasty battle had been avoided.

The last beast climbed the steps. At the top, it turned and gazed over the moon landscape. To Rufus, its gaze seemed to stop precisely at him and then, most strange of all, it waved. Rufus wanted to charge at the intruder. Who were these creatures to violate the king's land, treat it as their own and then feel brave enough to wave at Rufus without a care in the world? The young prince was incensed and probably would have done something rash had the door of the craft not already sealed shut.

Rufus stood perplexed. How had the intruders not seen them? They were just so close. Even the best hiding place couldn't contain all of the army. Yes, they had been quiet but the creatures had nearly been upon them. It was a mystery. Were they invisible to the invaders? It would certainly seem that way and a young Rufus was very thankful for the fact, as discovery would have led to a disaster.

King Rufus woke from his trance with a start. He picked up the knife at his side and threw it directly into the coloured rectangle of material above his fireplace. It was the same material from all those years ago but with lots of holes in it. All of the holes had been made by Rufus and his knife; he wanted revenge. For years, dreams and nightmares had penetrated the old king's sleep. Rufus often had dreams worse than his father's, about the Moon being consumed in fire, set alight by those strange creatures. He vowed that he would strike first and the invaders would never again set foot on the Moon.

CHAPTER NINE

On returning to the castle and towns, the old king had put his best scientists and philosophers to work to discover the who, what and why of the visitation. The most common theory was that the intruders had come from the patterned planet. Rufus believed this theory and wanted to have his revenge. For years, he planned to rule both planets so that the people of the patterned planet would bow at the mention of his name.

Following on from his father, Rufus also studied old books and texts searching for clues. He studied the patterned planet when he could and became familiar with its changing moods. He spent hours peering up at the planet through the most powerful telescopes on the Moon. Occasionally, he believed he could see things moving, but didn't trust himself, blaming those movements on tricks of the eye caused by staring through the lens for too long.

Early one morning, after spending the entire night in the moon library archives, Rufus found what he had been searching for – the answer to his dreams. Ever since that day he had been planning his vengeance and now his plans were near completion. The wheels had been set in motion, the cogs whirred, the date was set, and he believed that nothing could now stop him. All that was left was to assemble his finest people to form the initial landing party. An outer perimeter would first need to be secured so that Rufus could lead his amassed army against the violators. Rufus really felt that the intruders, from many years ago, had violated his land.

Unfortunately, shortly after those events, the old king succumbed to illness and died. Rufus blamed the invasion for the stress and strain that led to his father's death. This was yet another reason for the hatred that burned inside him for the colourful planet. Most of the Moon was shrouded in grey gloom and Rufus yearned for a world of colour much like his garden paradise, a garden that cost a considerable fortune in both creating and the current upkeep. To have a whole world of colour at his fingertips was so enticing, Rufus could hardly control his patience.

Now that his plan was coming together so nicely, selecting the finest people to undertake the invasion remained a puzzle. He needed a variety of skilled people who were the best of their respective fields. He wanted the finest swordsmen, the most skilled archers, the best rope walkers, the strongest and bravest soldiers.

Rufus pondered how he could choose the best people and how he could bring them all together. Suddenly, the king had a eureka moment. A light came on in his head and he jumped up, shouting, "I have it!"

Elated, Rufus quickly opened the crusty dusty old tome

on his desk. The pages were well worn but the book opened to the page containing pictures of the stones positioned in a complete circle. Rufus stroked the picture. "Soon my babies," he cooed.

The next morning, when his servants came in, they found the king fast asleep with his head on the book.

CHAPTER TEN

Molly, Pod, Mank and Ratabat awoke with the rising sun. Molly stretched her aching bones and rose slowly. They made a quick breakfast, packed up camp and were soon ready for the long trek home. It was early afternoon when they finally reached the outskirts of the Fogey's.

As they approached the edge of the ramshackle neighbourhood, Pod hurriedly made his excuses and began to run off, leaving Molly and Mank (and Ratabat, who was sleeping in Molly's breast pocket) to approach the Sate on their own. Molly, annoyed again at Pod's sudden disappearance, called after him but Pod merely raised a hand, waved and shouted, "Goodbye."

Unbeknown to Molly, Chunky, the Moon Monkey, who was slightly more intelligent than the average Moon Monkey, had discovered the whereabouts of Molly's neighbourhood. However, he had not discovered her actual house, which was well hidden from the street and from prying eyes.

Molly walked straight into a trap and the first she knew

about it was when Hunky, Chunky's right-hand man, leapt from the shadows and used his big feet to trip Molly up. Suddenly, Molly had four Moon Monkeys on her, one on each arm and leg. Once his quarry was secure, Chunky stepped out of the shadows and gave Molly a swift and painful kick in the ribs. Mank rushed to Molly's defence, but he was swiftly kicked into touch. The Moon Monkeys certainly could kick and Mank flew a good distance before landing heavily on his head with a shriek. The unfortunate Mank was knocked unconscious. Molly, meanwhile, was in the process of having her legs and hands tightly tied.

"I'm not so stupid now," hissed Chunky.

Molly was then roughly thrown into an old fishing net, which smelled rather bad.

Slung onto the back of the biggest Moon Monkey in the gang, Molly was roughly carried to the moozer, the regular haunt of Scarro. It now looked as if Scarro would finally have his revenge. The situation looked dire for Molly. Mank was nowhere to be seen, Pod had disappeared and Molly was tightly bound hand and foot.

After a very uncomfortable trip, she was unceremoniously dumped on the ground at the moozer's side entrance. This was a little quieter than the main entrance and was generally used by the establishment's more unsavoury characters. The Moon Monkeys took great pleasure in kicking and poking the suffering Molly before they disappeared through the door. Molly was left alone. Believing that she was going nowhere soon, Chunky didn't see the need for a guard. Although she struggled and wriggled, Molly felt resigned to the punishment. She knew that it wouldn't be good and might involve the loss of her limbs or worse. If only she could reach the Nitsplitter, she could cut the ropes that bound her and be free.

However, the more she wriggled, the tighter the restraints became.

She lay helpless, bedraggled and more than a little sore from the rough treatment she had received. Pausing for breath before another attempt to free herself, Molly suddenly became aware of movement in her breast pocket. Ratabat. The tiny creature slowly crawled out of the pocket. It seemed to know that its new friend was in trouble and in need of help. It began to crawl down Molly's arm. Once at her wrists, it began to chew on the bindings that held Molly firm. Although its teeth were only small, they were razor sharp.

Little by little, the rope restraining Molly began to fray. It seemed an age, but the tiny teeth were having an impact. Soon, between Ratabat's teeth and Molly straining and wriggling, the rope began to loosen and she released her hands from the frayed rope. Now that her hands were free, Molly could release the Nitsplitter from her boot. It soon made mincemeat of the remaining ropes and the fishing net and Molly was free. She scooped Ratabat up and gave the little creature a quick kiss before replacing it in her pocket.

By the time Scarro and Chunky reappeared, Molly was nowhere to be seen. Scarro was furious and he gave Chunky a swift right hook to the ear. Chunky fell to the ground and began to cry. This was not a good look in front of the other

Moon Monkeys, who looked aghast. No one had ever felled Chunky, the strongest Moon Monkey ever. Rolling in the dirt, Chunky's ear rang and he hated that little girl called Molly, more than ever.

By now, Molly had returned to the relative safety of the Sate and was, at that moment, in a rusty old tub, trying to soothe her aching body. She had fed Ratabat and Mank had returned, scratching his aching head. Not being particularly partial to the cleaning properties of water, Mank perched on Molly's raised knees, seeking attention for his own aches and pains. Once in bed and feeling relaxed for the first time in a while, Molly began to drift off.

CHAPTER ELEVEN

After a good night's sleep, Molly felt refreshed and her pains were slowly easing. After a swift breakfast of mouldy bread and homemade rat sausages, she was ready for the day's adventures. Mank was also feeling much better. He had eaten the breakfast leftovers and had twice tried to eat Ratabat – in a friendly way, or so Molly hoped. With her belly almost full for once, Molly began to clean her home as best she could.

The next few days were uneventful and she saw neither Chunky nor, worryingly, Pod. Both had their own problems, of which Molly was unaware. The Moon Monkeys and, in particular, Hunky, were now questioning Chunky's authority. Chunky blamed this on Molly and his hatred for her grew. Pod, meanwhile, had returned to his father's house where he was currently experiencing Angel's wrath. Although not at all happy, Pod was pleased that he could check up on the twins.

Molly was worried about Pod's continued absence and

spent many hours searching his regular haunts, but to no avail. When not searching for Pod, she made little trinkets and jewellery from her own and other people's rubbish. She was always surprised by the things that people threw away and she was able to turn many disused objects to her advantage. When she had time, she tried to sell her items at the moon market and, after a couple of lonely quiet days, she had collected and made enough to try her luck at the next morning's market.

The next morning, at the misty break of day, Molly set off to grab a little space at the market. She quickly set out her wares on a dusty old sheet she had found en route. It was not a very productive morning and she sold only a couple of her finest pieces. She was cold, bored and ready to call it a day when out the corner of her eye she spotted Pod. He was loaded down with baskets filled with fine produce from the market. Struggling to carry such a load, he staggered down the road, concentrating hard and desperately trying not to drop anything. Because of this, he failed to see that Molly was staring directly at him. She couldn't help but wonder what Pod was doing, where he had acquired the money to buy all that produce and, more importantly, where exactly he was going with it. She decided to follow Pod and get to the bottom of this mystery.

Molly set off at a leisurely pace. Even if he had seen her, Pod had no chance to escape her as he struggled with his load. After some time, Pod began to leave the poor quarters and move into a more affluent area. Who did Pod know in this area? wondered Molly. But Pod didn't hang around here. He walked through areas with ever bigger and ever grander houses. Molly had never visited this part of the Moon and she was in awe. Apart from the king's palace, Molly had never seen dwellings so big.

Pod began to slow as he came to a huge gate. The gate slowly opened and Pod disappeared through it. As soon as he went through, the gate quickly began to close. Molly shook her head in frustration. What the hell was going on? She was determined to find out, but how would she get in? She walked past the gate and began to search the wall for signs of weakness that would allow entry. She hadn't walked far before she saw a huge moontree, a very special event in itself. These very rare trees had an almost spiritual existence and were generally only found in the wealthiest of gardens. Here, one was growing on the side of the road. It was obviously old and it shivered, shiny in the pale moonlight. As was the tradition, the moontree was decorated with ribbons and candles. But it wasn't the tree's beauty and splendour that attracted Molly's attention. Some of the huge tree's branches touched and reached out over the wall and into the property beyond. It was illegal to harm this sacred tree, so the owner of the house could do nothing to prevent the intrusion of the tree onto their land. For an experienced acrobat like Molly, it offered perfectly easy access.

Before long, she was scaling the huge branches. She offered a prayer to the tree gods and could feel the ancient mystical power course through the branches. She shimmied along the limbs and was soon on the outer edges of the tree and then over the wall and into the grounds of the property.

Silently, she dropped to the floor and began to look about. She was on a well-manicured lawn. Hiding behind a shed at the bottom of the garden, she poked her head out and gazed up at the house. It was huge and ancient. Only the grandest and richest of people lived above the ground and this house had three floors. Large ornate windows, half covered by huge drapes and old-fashioned swags and tails, looked out onto the gardens. The curtains were so thick that if the sun was literally outside the window, it would not shine through.

Molly crept silently towards the slightly ajar back door. As she got closer, she heard a raised angry voice. Some poor unfortunate soul was being roundly berated by this unseen person. Molly peered through the gap in the door and what she saw broke her heart. Pod, loaded with baskets filled with shopping, was being beaten across the back of the legs by a horrid woman wielding a belt. He was in obvious pain but could not move or drop his load for fear of the bags and their contents flying all over the floor.

Angel was unhappy with Pod this time because he had forgotten to buy something from the market. "What will your father have for his tea now, you stupid boy? You know he always has moonbeam fish on a Friday." Her face was purple with rage and looked as if it might explode. The commotion had awoken the twins and their cries added to the noise and tension. "Now look what you have done, you imbecile. You have upset the babies. Now you are in real trouble."

Pod could hold on no longer and he dropped all the

bags to the floor. Vegetables, fruit, meats and cheese flew across the floor. Although it seemed impossible, the mad Angel was getting even worse. She grabbed a particularly vicious-looking meat cleaver from the kitchen worktop and began to advance on the stricken Pod.

Molly could take no more and she pushed the door open. "Leave him alone, you evil witch," she screamed at the woman while picking up a loose lemoon and launching it at the woman's head.

It hit Angel squarely between the eyes and she staggered. She put out an arm to steady herself and grabbed hold of a large saucepan containing Oodle's and Poodle's tea. The saucepan wobbled and flew into the air. It seemed to turn of its own accord and promptly landed on Angel's already bruised head. A sticky smelly gloop began to drip down her face. Molly, and even Pod, burst out laughing and the twins gurgled with delight. Angel was ready to kill and she shook with uncontrollable rage. She grabbed a knife and, slipping and sliding on the wet floor, advanced on Pod. Mank, who had been watching the events unfold from behind the door, suddenly leapt onto Angel's head and began to lap at the mushed food with his prickly tongue. Angel thrashed about wildly as her legs began to lose purchase on the slippery floor. In an instant, her feet were behind her ears as her derrière hit the floor with a rather loud thump.

"Time to get out of here, Pod," screamed Molly.

They raced towards the door. As they ran out, Pod grabbed a leaflet that was sitting on the sideboard. They raced down the road, with Angel's screams and obscenities ringing in their ears. They didn't stop running until they had reached the relative safety of the Sate. Once inside, they promptly fell to the floor, breathless. When they caught their breath, they both burst out laughing.

"God, that was funny," said Molly.

"Yes," replied Pod, "but I am in dead trouble now and she will not let this rest!"

"Don't worry about that now," Molly said. "Let's hope she calms down and who the moon dunny was she? You clearly knew her and she definitely knew a lot about you."

Molly had so many questions. Whose house was it? Who were the twin babies? Molly, almost shouting at Pod, blurted all these thoughts out in one go. Pod went bright red, shrugged his shoulders and his eyes went moist.

Wiping his face with the grubby collar of his dirty coat, Pod replied, "Please, Molly, I just can't, not right now, please, it hurts too much."

Molly, realising that her friend was in some distress, rushed to give him a hug. As she squeezed Pod hard, something fell out of his top pocket and fluttered to the floor. Pod, recovering quickly from his anguish, picked up the flyer from the floor and gradually unfolded it. Excitedly, Molly grabbed the leaflet from Pod.

"What is it?" Molly asked.

Pod, who was feeling a bit better and pleased that he could quickly distract Molly from his predicament, couldn't contain himself any longer and didn't give Molly time to read the leaflet before he eagerly blurted out, "It's the king and he is having a Grand Royal Tournament. It will take place over two weeks and cover all aspects of combat, skill, strength and fighting. He is calling it the event of the century!"

"So?" said Molly. "What is that to us? We will never get a seat and why are you so excited?"

"Because," Pod replied, pausing for dramatic effect, "we will not need a seat. I have registered *you* to compete!"

Molly dropped the leaflet in shock. "You what?" she exclaimed. "How? What? *Why*?"

"Think about it," said Pod. "You are the best crater walker I know and the leaflet says the prizes will be awesome. I have entered you into the crater joust. I know you can win!"

"Are you crazy?" muttered Molly. "I will never beat Carnaverous the Great."

"Think about it," said Pod. "You don't even know that he exists and just think if you win, we will be rich!!!"

"What do you mean *we*?" jested Molly. Feeling the excitement mount, she began to feel butterflies creep up from her stomach, as nervous adrenalin rushed through her body. She started to believe Pod's words and, deep down, knew that she was very good, if not the best.

With shaking hands, Molly picked up the leaflet to read. Pod was correct. The king intended to hold a tournament with huge and out-of-this-world prizes, although the leaflet didn't say exactly what. She imagined the untold riches that her victory would bring. "Wait!" she said, as she clutched her hair and began to pull at it wildly. "This states that the event is only three weeks away! I will never be ready!"

"You are ready now," Pod assured her, as he tried to calm the excited Molly who had suddenly gone into a state of nervous meltdown.

"Quick! I must practise! I need to train!" she exclaimed.

"Tomorrow," said Pod. "It is getting late and I am hungry and we can spend all day tomorrow practising if you really want!"

Slowly coming to her senses, Molly knew that Pod was right. Indeed, her stomach was beginning to rumble too. Together with Mank, who had reappeared at the mention of food, and Ratabat in Molly's pocket, they set off in search of food.

CHAPTER TWELVE

Molly was up bright and early the next morning, ready and eager to start. She and Pod spent the day practising; time and time again, she stretched the Rord across a large moon crater. Once in position, she then crossed the thin taut Rord, performing twists, jumps and acrobatic back-flips as she did so. She landed smoothly on the slightly swaying Rord each time.

Her skill, poise and balance left Pod in awe and appreciation; he could only gape with his mouth wide open as the lithe Molly performed a particularly complex double back-flip, landing perfectly on the Rord.

Hours and then days of practice passed and soon the week had flown by. The two friends trained in peace, undisturbed by anyone else. Molly briefly wondered what had happened to Chunky and his gang. In addition, they'd had no trouble from the palace guards or the army, as they were all busy preparing for the tournament.

What Molly didn't know was that Chunky was also in training. He had entered into the strong man competition, believing that if he could win then he could regain the respect of Hunky and the rest of the Moon Monkey gang. The officials had been reluctant to let Chunky register, but when threatened with a Moon Monkey boot and, after a hasty look at the rule book, the steward could find no reason not to allow a Moon Monkey to enter.

Molly was, therefore, fully focused and trained for long periods each day with little or no disturbance. Once, she was forced to quickly hide when Chunky ran past – the Moon Monkey also zoomed round an unsuspecting soldier, who happened to stare at Chunky for a little too long and received a quick slap around the ear for the pleasure – but that was it really.

Molly was pleased that Chunky was in such a hurry as it could well have been her ear.

CHAPTER THIRTEEN

A week before the big event, Molly, who was by now almost hyperventilating with excitement, took some time off to view the tournament preparations. She was overwhelmed by the size and grandeur of the arenas, and it seemed that no expense had been spared. The king was obviously intent on making the Royal Tournament the greatest spectacle that the Moon had seen for many a year. Huge stands encircled all the venues to allow the maximum number of people to view the events.

Molly crept towards the crater where the crater joust event would take place. The stand and arena looked huge and intimidating; the hairs on the back of her neck stood up. She could almost hear the roar of the crowd, chanting her name as she held aloft a huge golden cup that glinted brightly in the moonbeams.

Without warning, Molly was brought back to reality as a guard gave her a swift clip on the ear.

"Oi, you little urchin. Get out of here," cried the guard. "You are not allowed here. It's restricted."

Molly didn't need to be told twice; she took flight with her ears ringing and the cheering crowds growing silent in her mind.

The guard, who couldn't be bothered to give chase, merely mumbled, "Bloody peasants." Like many in the army, he couldn't wait for the tournament to be over and life to return to normal, which, to this particular guard, meant sleeping on watch and eating a lot!

Large temporary camps were being set up with great care and ceremony around the tournament grounds, with each visiting group attempting to outdo the others in grandeur and colour. There were the silver men of the far side, who were huge, toned and muscled and who shimmered silver in the moonlight. They were a proud nation, recognised for their strength and fighting skills. They generally kept to themselves but those who entered their territory unannounced never lived to tell the tale. From the mountains came the mwarves, distant relatives of the ancient moon miners. They were squat and strong, and skilled with hammer and axe. Molly tried to keep away from the mwarves. She still remembered the first time she had come face to face with one when the Rord, which was wrapped around her waist, began to vibrate and glow. The mwarf closest to her went into a strange trance and his eyes widened to the size of saucers. Molly ran off before anything else occurred. Who knew what would have happened? All Molly knew was that the mwarves didn't mix well with other people. In the run-up to the tournament, the palace guards were kept busy splitting up drunken fights outside the city's moozers. The mwarves took particular offence at the silver men; the mere sight of them seemed to drive the mwarves into a fighting frenzy. The citizens of the city eagerly awaited the meetings of these two tribes in the arena.

Molly was most frightened by the strange, eerie Samhain Mage, who wore long cloaks, and kept their faces hidden from view. They walked serenely around the camps, occasionally unleashing sudden powerful blasts. White balls of lightning shot from their heavily tattooed hands, obliterating whatever or whoever got in the way. The trees and buildings around their camp were taking a right battering. Finally, the king, dismayed by the amount of damage, gave them one of the arenas as a special practice area, in an effort to prevent further damage.

Molly was most intrigued by a rather plainly adorned tent, with tent panels covered in strange and colourless heliographic pictures and ancient runes. A street urchin who Molly knew as an acquaintance had told her that this was the camp of the one and only Carnaverous the Great. Molly tried to get a closer look at the camp but each time she got close an armed guard blocked her way. When Molly told Pod, he shrugged his shoulders and said, "So what if it is? If you are lucky, you will meet him in the competition." Molly got his point and tried to put the great man to the back of her mind, although she kept an almost constant watch on the strange camp in the hope of glimpsing him.

Molly had never seen so many people of all the nationalities of the Moon. It would seem that the whole world had heard of the king's tournament. As well as the contestants, there were a great many who had come to view the spectacle. In addition, of course, there were the profiteers who recognised the potential for big financial rewards from such an event. The city was full of pickpockets, beggars and thieves. It was a dangerous and exciting time but one needed to stay sharp.

CHAPTER FOURTEEN

At last, it was the first day of the Royal Tournament. Molly was fully awake before dawn. She found it impossible to sleep and lay in bed twisting and turning. Her entire body tingled with anticipation and excitement. The day began with a huge procession of all the contestants throughout the city.

Molly walked alongside the other crater joust contestants, who came from all parts of the Moon. In the midst of the crater walkers was a carriage carried on the shoulders of dock slaves. Molly found herself next to the carriage. It was completely shrouded in darkness, and thick curtains covered the windows. There was not even a chink for Molly to see through, but she could feel the hum of magic emanating from the dark interior. She tried to move even closer to the carriage but an invisible wall of energy hummed and pushed her back. Although she wasn't certain, she thought it must be the carriage of Carnaverous the Great. How she wished she could talk to or even get a glimpse of the great man.

Almost every contestant waved a coloured flag stating their nationality and their tournament event. The colour, grandeur, pomp and ceremony were on a scale never seen before. The spectators, ten deep on either side of the road, waved, cheered and shouted the names of their favourite competitors. The sense of expectation and excitement was palpable. Some of the young bucks, a little overzealous after spending a little too long in the moozer, kept the king's guards occupied.

The column of contestants stretched as far as the eye could see as they made their way to the main arena. Group by group they filed into the newly built stadium, waving flags and singing songs from times long past. Slowly but surely, they were directed and moved into position in front of the royal enclosure. The king would arrive soon, give his speech and declare the games open. The crowd grew quiet as the select band played the royal fanfare followed by the king's national anthem. Suddenly, the king appeared from behind huge ornate banners and began his speech. Announcing how proud he was, he launched into a long rambling speech about patriotism.

Molly was soon bored and began to look around. Judging by the increase in whispers and jostling, it was clear that most of the crowd felt the same. Everyone was keen to get started. Luckily, one of the king's advisors picked up on the atmosphere and gave the king a swift nudge. Taking the hint, the king swiftly moved on and the crowd erupted into a huge cheer when he told of the riches and rewards the winners could expect. Finally, he declared the games open, that serious competition would begin tomorrow and, for tonight, the Moon would party! A twenty-one-gun salute was fired and the cheering of the crowd reached a crescendo. Molly had to cover her ears. If they had been any louder, she was sure the patterned planet would have heard them.

A few in the crowd began to sing a battle song of old. Their voices were quiet at first, but everyone in the arena was singing this song of loyalty, bravery and honour. Molly felt the hairs on the back of her neck stick up and blood and pride pump through her veins. Everyone felt the same and the opening ceremony of the Royal Tournament was talked about for many years.

Out of the masses emerged Pod and Mank. Ratabat popped its head out of its pocket home. But for Molly, the joy was short-lived. She felt a piercing glare on her back and when she turned around, she glimpsed Chunky giving her evil eyes. Molly was startled to discover that he too was a contestant. But any horrid thoughts she had were soon swept away as Pod grabbed her and began to dance, if indeed Pod's movements could be called dancing.

CHAPTER FIFTEEN

Molly awoke the next morning both excited and a little fuzzy-headed; Pod had managed to steal a flagon of moonshine. While the two had been awestruck by the evening's entertainment it was now down to business. Molly was due at the arena at noon for the first round of competition. She spent some time limbering up but felt as ready as she would ever be. She knew that her first opponent was a young local boy from a village close to the city. He was capable and strong but had a weakness in his left leg. Molly knew this because she had occasionally seen him hunting moonster bats. She often watched other hunters in action. Who knew what she could learn from them, that would then lead to a bigger dinner?

To while away the hours until her bout, Molly went to the main arena, where the first round of many of the games was already underway. She couldn't believe her eyes when she saw Chunky standing tall and proud, pounding his chest in readiness for battle. Hiding among the crowd, Molly stood, fascinated, with battle about to commence. The contest proved a little one-sided, as the large and imposing Chunky faced a poor villager from the moon wastes.

In the first round, Chunky properly battered the poor man, at least twice nearly separating his head from his shoulders. Bravely, his opponent managed to make it to the second round, although it soon became apparent that the outcome would be the same as the first. Molly could not stand to watch anymore and moved towards the poor man's corner. At the end of the second round, battered, bloodied and bruised, Chunky's opponent approached his corner and sat down. Molly took the opportunity to quickly whisper something in the man's ear. Although the outcome was never in doubt, the man managed to last a further five rounds, lived to tell the tale and even inflicted some damage on Chunky's nose, all thanks to Molly's advice.

The time leading up to her contest seemed to drag but finally it was Molly's turn to enter the games. She dressed in her finest battle gear, which was an old war tunic she had found at the market. She had patched up the holes and added ribbons to give the drab garment some colour. Nervous excitement coursed through her body. Unfortunately, the contest rules stipulated that all contestants had to use the same standard and grade of rope for crater crossing. Molly kept the Rord safely concealed around her waist, as she couldn't bear to leave it on the side while she competed. Its presence comforted her and she could feel its magic course around her waist.

At long last, Molly faced the young lad across the huge competition crater. In a real battle, the loser would disappear into the crater depths, never to be seen again. However, as this was a competition, the loser, though likely battered and bruised, would fall into a safety net stretched across the crater.

Molly stood at the edge of the crater, stretching on her toes. She was as ready as she ever could be. Suddenly, the huge klaxon sounded, a roar erupted from the crowd and Molly's competition began. Stepping onto the rope, she took a few seconds to familiarise herself with its strange feel under her toes. She wobbled for an instant but then her instincts kicked in. She felt alive, with nothing but the air all around her and the thin rope beneath her. Gradually, she moved towards the centre and her opponent. The longer she was on the rope, the more confident she became. Finally, she allowed herself to look at the young lad who approached her. He was muscular and fit but, when Molly looked at his young face, she saw beads of sweat, a nervous tick and an intense look of concentration. Seeing him like this gave Molly a surge of confidence and, for the first time, she knew that she could actually win.

Each contestant carried a regulation javarod. This fighting pole was sharp and pointed on one end to slice and stab and had a hook on the other, to hook a leg and unbalance an opponent. Molly began to spin her javarod around and around, faster and faster, until it became a blur. The crowd hushed, cooed and oooed at her obvious skill. Her young opponent stared at her and almost lost his balance as he admired her poise and grace. However, he quickly regained his composure, launched an attack and quickly thrust the javarod straight into Molly's whirring javarod.

There was a sudden jarring as stick clashed against stick and Molly was knocked completely off balance. She found herself wobbling dangerously on the rope, her toes scrambling to maintain their grip. Suddenly, she launched into a back-flip, floated high in the air and landed on the rope with poise and agility. As she regained her composure, she knew that she could not take anything for granted and needed to concentrate at all times. This was no place to show off.

With renewed determination, she began to advance on her opponent. He had gained confidence and believed that he had the fight won. He charged towards her. The two javarod poles struck with a clang. Molly was again pushed back; the young lad was certainly strong. She managed to jab the javarod into his shoulder, halting his advance. He howled in pain as blood seeped through his taut top. The pain seemed to send him mad and he waved his javarod in temper and frustration rather than with control. Molly easily dodged his amateur attempts to overthrow her.

His manic efforts were causing the lad to tire. Just as Molly realised she had him, the klaxon sounded for the end of the first round. Returning to her side of the crater, she grabbed a quick drink and listened to Pod's kind-hearted advice. However, she knew exactly what she had to do and that was finish the fight. The break had refreshed her opponent. Glancing over at him, Molly could tell that he had regained his composure. She was worried that he would have more stamina the longer the contest went on; plus, she knew she would need her energy for later rounds. It was time to finish this. She approached the rope with a grim determination.

The klaxon sounded for the second round. Molly advanced to the centre with precision. She was ready and in the zone. Her opponent knew it and she could smell his fear. As they gently tapped javarods, as a mutual show of respect, the young lad was already retreating and on the back foot. Molly swung to attack the injured shoulder again, but it was a bluff. Her opponent shifted his weight and stick to protect his injured side. Slightly unbalanced and unable to protect his weaker left leg, Molly took this opportunity to stab the javarod directly into his left knee. The leg buckled and gave way, and any chance of victory was now well out of his reach. His arms windmilled wildly and he quickly disappeared into the abyss, bouncing a couple of times on the safety net before coming to a gentle rest. His knee was dislocated and he had a flesh wound on his shoulder, but his injuries were not life-threatening.

Molly spun on the rope in a victory pirouette, then back-flipped along the rope to the crater edge. She knew she was showing off but she felt so good about her first competition success that she couldn't help herself. Once back on firm ground, Pod and Mank rushed to her. Pod swept her up in a big bear hug and spun her around.

Realising what he was doing and in front of a huge crowd of onlookers, he sheepishly put Molly down, saying, in a slightly embarrassed tone, "Ahem, well done, Moll."

Even Ratabat had caught the competition fever.

It appeared from Molly's pocket, flapping its small wings and squawking in excitement. Suddenly, Pod produced a large moon money note; he quickly explained to Molly that he had put a few coins of his meagre savings on a bet for Molly to win, he knew she would and it was a certainty. Molly, annoyed with this, began to berate Pod but soon her temper began to dissipate when Pod told Molly about all the lovely items he intended to buy.

"Let's celebrate and get something to eat," he shouted as he rushed towards the food market stalls. He was intent on enjoying his moon note and used it to splash out on all manner of moon delicacies.

They ate crocopig burgers, moon nuts, and exotic and rare moorab. Molly had never eaten half of the things that Pod was buying but the moorab was extra special. A moorab was a crab-like creature with eight eyes and four large pincers on each side of its body. The creature had the ability to turn around inside its shell allowing front to become back and vice versa. With its claws for protection on each side, it was a notoriously difficult creature to catch. However, the delicate meat within made the effort of catching it worthwhile. Molly couldn't get enough of it, but she saved some room for a couple of slices of homemade lemoon cake.

Feeling quite full and a little sick, Molly settled against a large tree for a five-minute nap. Suddenly, she was roughly shaken awake by Pod who urged her to rise from her slumber. She had slept for two hours and was now due back in the competition crater for her next round. Molly darted between the crowds as she desperately tried to shake out the sleep. She was ready with only seconds to spare when the klaxon sounded for the second round.

Nervous and a little unsteady, Molly ventured out across the crater on the taut rope. Unprepared, aching, full and still feeling a little sick, Molly was concerned about her second-round chances. She made a vow that should she be fortunate enough to get through this round, she would be fully focused, battle-ready and prepared for future bouts. Luckily, her opponent had also been celebrating and had spent most of the time between the rounds in the moozer.

Full of moonshine, the crusty old man facing Molly stepped onto the rope, managed to almost reach Molly, wobbling all the way, raised his javarod to attack and promptly fell off. Laughing as he disappeared into the crater, the only damage inflicted was to his pride and a very sore head. Molly was through to the third round and the second day without having to raise her rod in anger. She couldn't believe her luck and truly felt that fortune was smiling on her that evening.

When she returned to the land, Pod rushed forward to chastise her for her lack of preparation, although he was secretly proud that she had made it to day two, which was quite an achievement. The competition had also gone well for Chunky who breezed into day two and was a firm favourite, having landed most of his opponents in the casualty tent. Both tired and eager to be prepared for the next day, Molly and Chunky, unbeknown to each other, climbed into their beds, ready for a good night's sleep. Molly immediately fell straight into a deep and contented sleep.

CHAPTER SIXTEEN

The next morning dawned crisp and clear, promising a stunning day ahead. Molly awoke, stretched and rose briskly. After washing in the communal showers that the king had kindly provided for the competitors, she felt refreshed and clean. This was a rare feeling and Molly enjoyed the privilege of hot water. Ready and raring to go, Molly picked up the Rord, and set off to do some early morning exercises. On her return, she caught the welcoming whiff of crisping crocopig. Pod had saved some from the previous day and was busy cooking it on an open fire.

"Come on," he said. "Got to keep your energy up."

Molly's stomach rumbled. "I'm starving," she cried, suddenly realising how hungry she was. She would need all her strength for the day ahead.

Meanwhile, Chunky was preparing for his first bout of the day. He would be first in the fighting arena that morning. His opponent was a half giant from the far side of the Moon. Although only a half giant, the man was still huge. He was bigger even than Chunky, who had his work cut out to progress further. The klaxon sounded and the two combatants slowly circled each other, testing each other and patiently looking for their opponent's weaknesses. Round after round the two battered each other, inflicting horrible injuries.

In the final round, just as it was looking like a stalemate, Chunky mustered one last surge of energy, swung his big heavy fist and clean knocked the half giant off his feet. Out for the count and unable to rise from the ground, the half giant finally succumbed to the might of Chunky, who roared and beat his chest in victory.

CHAPTER SEVENTEEN

At the crater, Molly faced a master, someone almost as good as Carnaverous the Great. Molly knew she was in for quite the battle. Her opponent, Christos, was a hardened campaigner with a great deal of experience. He was tough and uncompromising and had demolished all of his opponents in the previous day's competition. Molly approached him with caution; she had no intention of following those that had gone before her. More defensive than attacking, Molly skipped and dodged a dogged attack from Christos. She ducked and dived, spun and jumped, using all her skill and balance to remain securely on the rope.

Only once did he break through her defence, landing a hefty whack on Molly's thigh but, although a little sore, no real damage was done. By the end of the first round, Molly was breathing hard and sweating.

Pod rushed to her side, wiped her brow and gave her some refreshing juice. "You must attack, Molly," he said. "You can't keep absorbing his attacks. He will finally get through."

"I know," Molly replied. "It's just that he is so good. I'll never win!"

"Come on, Molly," shouted Pod. "Believe!"

With Pod's sound advice in her ears, Molly gritted her teeth in determination and returned to the centre of the crater. Almost at once Christos advanced on her. As he feigned one way, Molly swerved to avoid the imaginary attack only to receive his javarod squarely in the eye. She was lucky that it wasn't the sharp end but the damage was still substantial. Blood oozed from her eye and it began to swell. Christos, sensing victory, was on the attack again. This time, the sharp end glanced past Molly's head, narrowly missing separating Molly's ear from her head. Before she could move, Christos spun the javarod around and hooked Molly's leg. Balancing on one leg, Molly's position was critical; her contest was over unless she took drastic action.

Suddenly, Molly flipped over onto her hands so that she was in the handstand position, facing straight down into the abyss. She bounced up and down, causing Christos to halt his attack to concentrate on maintaining his own balance. Once Molly had gained enough momentum, she launched herself up into the air and over the top of the confused Christos. Nimbly landing on her feet behind him, she managed to jab her opponent before he could turn around. Christos slumped forward. Molly had finally inflicted some pain and had drawn blood. It was a small victory which only served to make her attacker angrier.

Snarling, Christos turned and advanced on Molly again, spinning the pole at lightning speed and whacking her squarely across the side. Winded, Molly had to crouch down on all fours, clutching the rope. Christos advanced again. Molly knew that she wouldn't survive another brutal attack. She curled into a ball and waited for the final assault; Christos raised the javarod over his head and was just about to strike the winning blow when the klaxon sounded for the end of the second round. Molly had never heard a more welcoming sound and quickly took advantage of the break to crawl towards Pod and relative safety, at least for a couple of minutes.

Pod tried his best to encourage and push Molly towards just one final effort, but even he was worried. Molly's eye was battered and swollen and her vision was severely restricted. She was bruised and bloody and her body ached all over. All too quickly her brief respite was over and the klaxon sounded for the start of the next round. She was in real danger of being eliminated from the competition but somehow, using strength she didn't know she had, she mounted the rope again.

Slowly approaching Christos on wobbly legs, she braced for another attack. She was not disappointed as her attacker's javarod swiftly prodded her in the stomach. She fell to her knees on the rope and it was then that Christos made his mistake. Thinking that the contest was won, he rushed towards Molly with the javarod raised above his head and his defences down. Molly, summoning her very last reserves of strength, swung her own javarod hard across Christos's knees.

With a look of complete shock and surprise, her

opponent's legs buckled and he tumbled forward, straight towards Molly. As he fell, he grabbed at Molly with a flaying arm, knocking her off balance. Suddenly the pair of them were headed towards the abyss and the safety net. Quickly and with some considerable skill, Molly reached out with her javarod and hooked the end over the tightrope.

By now, Christos had disappeared into the darkness and Molly was left hanging in the air, clinging to her javarod. Slowly, the swinging javarod began to steady. Molly clung on for her life but, as the pole stopped swaying, Molly began to inch her way towards the rope. Slowly, she reached out and grabbed the rope with her left hand. Painfully and carefully, she eased her bruised and damaged body back onto the rope. Encouraged by the cheers of the crowd, she edged her way along the rope back towards Pod and solid land. If she could get that far, the bout would be hers and she would have overcome the strongest opponent that she had ever fought on the rope. Every step to safety hurt and only by her sheer iron will, Molly dragged herself to safety. Her body protested every slight movement but gradually the distance between her and the crater edge diminished. With a final monumental effort, Molly stood and propelled herself towards the moon surface. She landed hard on the unforgiving ground and promptly collapsed. Although it hurt, Molly had never felt so relieved to hit the hard land.

Pod rushed to her and scooped her up in his arms. She was out for the count. Pod was very worried. She was in a bad way and would be in no shape to continue. Her competition was as good as over. He began to brush the hair from her face and whisper words of encouragement into her ear. A crowd had gathered around the stricken pair, eager to see the results of the battle.

Suddenly, a loud voice boomed, "Stand back, all of you. Give the girl some room."

It was not a voice to be messed with and the crowd parted to let a tall, hooded, cloaked figure through. The cloak shimmered in the moonlight and was covered in the same mysterious runes and arcane symbols as those on the alleged tent of Carnaverous the Great. If Molly had been conscious, she would have been ecstatic for it was, indeed, the legendary Carnaverous.

He knelt beside Molly and began to assess her injuries. "You fought well, little one, and you deserve your chance," he whispered in a voice that resonated with wisdom and power. He began to chant mysterious words that had a strange rhythm and music-like quality. Then, he clapped his hands twice. His hands began to glow and heat up. He ran them across her injuries, all the while chanting his incantations.

Although Molly didn't awaken, she began to warm up and relax, and her bones began to heal and mend. Her bruises began to noticeably fade, her swollen eye started to shrink back down and her cuts started to close up. After some time, Carnaverous turned to Pod and told him that Molly would be fine, but that she would sleep now until the morning. The great man then produced a vial filled with murky liquid, handed it to Pod and told him to rub the contents onto the worst of the injuries in the morning. With that, and a grand flap of his cloak, Carnaverous disappeared into the crowd again. Pod could only stare after him and scratch his head. Molly would never believe him and would be gutted to have been so close to her idol and yet know nothing about it. Pod gently carried the unconscious Molly back to their camp.

CHAPTER EIGHTEEN

However, Molly was not yet out of danger. Chunky was in the moozer celebrating reaching the final of his event. As he ordered yet another drink, he overheard a very interesting story concerning a young girl who had been beaten senseless and near death but had somehow overcome the odds to win. It had to be Molly, thought Chunky.

Slowly, through his slightly addled brain, which wasn't too bright even on a sober day, he began to form a murderous plan. If Molly was truly weakened and close to death, then what better time to finish her off than now, when she was in no state to offer resistance. Downing the drink he had just bought, Chunky set off for Molly's tent. Stealthily, he crept towards it, and stood outside, listening intently. Hearing no sound from inside the tent, he slowly entered. Molly lay sleeping on her bed, unaware of her impending doom. Pod was curled up and also sound asleep on a chair in the corner.

A wicked grin spread across Chunky's face. At last, he thought. After all this time and torment, he finally had his revenge. Sliding a knife from his sleeve, he poised to strike. He raised his massive arm and swiftly began to strike at the prone Molly. But rather than plunging deep into Molly's chest, the razor-sharp knife struck something hard and unforgiving. Chunky's arm shot back up in the air and the knife flew across the tent, landing harmlessly in a plant pot in the corner. Molly was surrounded by a bright golden halo, which glowed and shimmered in the dark tent.

"What?" screamed Chunky. "What magic is this?"

In a rage, he lifted his huge Moon Monkey foot and, using his incredible power, aimed a deadly stamp at Molly's head. Unfortunately, as soon as Chunky's foot connected with the glowing aura, it began to sizzle and burn, and the hairs on his foot turned black and singed. His entire body arched up into the air and he landed sprawled against the side of the tent.

All of this commotion had finally woken Pod from his deep sleep. He grabbed the nearest weapon to hand, which happened to be a night bedpan that he had stolen in case Molly was too ill to get to the public latrine. Weapon in hand, Pod began to whack the bedpan across the head of the shaken Chunky. This would not normally have bothered the thick-headed Chunky, but with his badly burnt foot and the mysterious aura of magic, the pounding he was now taking to his head made him choose the wisest course of action and he swiftly exited the tent.

The shocked Pod fell back into his chair. Once the initial surprise had worn off, he burst out laughing. The mighty Chunky fleeing the small waif-like Pod, with his head ringing, his foot burning and worrying thoughts in his head. Pod had no choice but to laugh. Molly would never ever believe him.

CHAPTER NINETEEN

The next morning broke cool and crisp. Molly awoke, stretched and yawned. Her body ached and she wasn't completely sure where she was. As she looked around and her vision began to clear, she saw the concerned face of Pod emerge out of the haze.

"Thank the great lord," he said. "You are back. How are you feeling? We were so worried."

"What wall did I crash into?" moaned Molly.

Pod suddenly produced the bottle and said, "Stay still. I need to apply this to your worst injuries." As he removed the stopper, a pungent odour quickly spread around the tent.

"Yuck. That's absolutely vile," screamed Molly. "What the Moon Monkey is it? It stinks worse than Chunky."

"Well," said Pod, "you won't believe me when I tell you!" He then replayed the strange events from the previous day.

Molly's eyes grew as wide as saucers and her jaw dropped in astonishment. Unbelievable, she thought, and I was completely unaware of everything. She was most upset at missing the opportunity to speak to and maybe even touch Carnaverous, although she acknowledged the role that Pod played and was vocal in her thanks and appreciation. "Carnaverous must have put a protection spell around me. That is what protected me," she whispered.

"Yes, that was my thought," said Pod. "Now, come on, time to drag yourself up. A public shower under the lunar falls will soon clear the cobwebs. We will put the potion on after you have showered and returned."

Gingerly, and with some considerable lingering pain, Molly lifted herself from the bed. Pod helped walk and carry Molly to the cold water shower.

"Do you mind," she protested. "I am a lady, don't you know! Please refrain from looking."

Sheepishly, Pod turned his back as Molly entered the freezing cold shower. At first, the freezing water was a shock to her tiny frame. The cold water plunged over the falls at a great rate, penetrating her pain. The cold soon had her blood flowing swiftly around her battered body.

Gradually, Molly began to feel refreshed and gingerly started stretching and flexing her bruised arms and legs. Finally, she couldn't avoid it any longer – it was time to apply the foul-smelling lotion, although only the holy moon mother knew what was in it.

Back at the tent, she lay on her bed and Pod began to warm his hands.

"Don't go getting any funny ideas," she said.

Feigning hurt, Pod replied, "Shut up. Would I? I'd rather stroke a moon snake. They have much softer skin."

Molly threw the lotion bottle at Pod's head, who luckily was deft enough to catch it. "Just get on with it," she sighed.

Once Pod removed the stopper all banter suddenly ceased; the lotion was truly foul. The tent filled with the aroma of the city sewers, only much worse. Holding his breath, Pod applied the ointment as quickly as he could. Molly lay stock still while he rubbed the stinky potion into her many bruises and wounds. Amazingly, once he had covered the very last bruise, Molly retched, jumped up and ran out of the stinking tent.

The potion works well then! thought Pod as he quickly replaced the stopper and rushed out after her.

Molly was transformed. Having been battered, bruised and one step from death, she now felt on top of the world. Suddenly, she launched into a routine of stunning flips and somersaults. "I am back. No one can stop me now," she screamed mid-air.

Pod could only stand and admire his friend. He wondered what that vile-smelling potion could possibly contain. Whatever it was, it must have been good because Molly was as ready as she ever would be for her semi-final later in the day.

Molly returned to Pod, exclaiming, "I'm starving."

The morning passed in a blur and Molly grew increasingly excited with each passing minute. The semi-final was approaching. She was intent on soaking up the atmosphere. Absorbing the smells and sounds of the pageantry, she felt alive and ready to fight the whole of the king's army if need be. For the first time, she believed that she could actually win. She wanted to make Carnaverous and her family proud.

She suddenly picked up the startled Mank and, despite numerous fleas jumping for their lives, Molly gave the disgruntled cat a huge hug and kiss. "Oh, Mank, I love you," she said.

Mank's reply was to fart in her face.

"Yuck," screamed Molly as she swiftly dropped the manky old cat. "You smell worse than that potion."

Those unfortunate enough to be close by held their noses and moved quickly on. Molly couldn't be sure whether she or the cat smelled worse!

CHAPTER TWENTY

The time was upon them and Molly was due to fight in the first semi-final. She quickly completed her warm-up routine and went through her final preparations. At last, after much fanfare, her name was announced and the crowd erupted. They had taken this strange little girl, who refused to give up, into their hearts and cheered her on with great enthusiasm. It was awe-inspiring.

Molly, slightly shocked, absorbed this feeling, love and power. She felt ten feet tall and ready to conquer the world. The colour and spectacle around her was almost overwhelming, the sights and smells overpowering her senses. She suddenly felt giddy and had to slow her breathing and regain control, ground herself and get ready for the fight ahead.

In all the hype and excitement, Molly had forgotten about her opponent and had no idea who she would be fighting. As she approached the rope, she looked up and straight at her opponent. Gulping, she had to take a second look. Facing her was a creature she had never seen before, although she had heard strange tales around the tournament camps.

The creature staring intently at Molly was Sally Lion Head, a strange-looking thing indeed. Sally had three legs which obviously gave her a huge advantage on the crater rope. She had a long flowing mane, which was where her lion head name came from. It looked very fluffy, but hidden within it were poisonous spikes and snakes. With a shake of her long neck, Sally Lion Head could shoot these poisonous spikes and snakes in any direction she desired, a feat that she had used to great effect in her previous round. The king's physicians had so far pulled twenty-nine such projectiles out of Sally's last opponent. Finally, to complete her armoury, Sally Lion Head had a fluffy tail, which helped aid her three legs for balance. Concealed under the fluff of the tail was a hard ball of bone that could smash heads for fun. She was a mighty and fearsome opponent, and a very tough combatant for Molly to overcome if she hoped to reach the final.

Molly should have feared for her life and been despondent, but she didn't feel like that at all. Instead, she felt rejuvenated, energised and completely at one with the task at hand. The starter klaxon sounded; Molly flowed out onto the crater centre, her tiny feet already at one with the rope. As she approached her contestant, a thought sprang to mind. *Remove one obstacle at a time and you will win*, her conscience told her firmly.

Her first task set, Molly approached Sally ready to attack the third leg. Swinging the javarod so fast it was a blur, she landed blow after blow on Sally's third leg. By the end of the first round, Sally was really struggling as the advantage of her extra leg was already greatly diminished. However, Sally hadn't reached the semi-final by giving up, and she was more prepared for round two. She landed a couple of painful blows on Molly who suddenly knew she was in a real scrap. By the time the klaxon sounded for the end of round two, Sally was ahead on blows landed. She had won the second round and the fight now stood at one round each.

As Molly rested during the break, quickly gulping at some fluid, her mind spoke to her again. *Attack the fluffy tail*, it whispered. Indeed, thought Molly. It was Sally's tail that had landed most of the damaging blows in the preceding round. Sally used her tail to great effect, spinning swiftly around on the rope as her tail lashed into her opponent. Molly quickly hatched a plan to destroy the tail but her timing would need to be precise if she were to successfully execute the attack.

The break ended all too soon and Molly was confronted by her opponent once again. Sally snarled and looked mean enough to make babies cry. Molly ignored her and began to concentrate on the attack ahead; her breathing was calm, her senses alert, and her blood flowed swiftly through every fibre of her body. She could feel the cold touch of the light moon breeze on the erect hairs on her arm; she was ready, her body coiled, poised. She recognised the signs and knew that Sally was preparing another spin. This was Molly's chance; the dangerous tail was coming in her direction. Sally spun around and the tail lashed out towards Molly. She leapt high into the air as the tail whipped by, inches below her legs, right where her head would have been. Hovering with superhuman strength, almost flying, Molly now had her chance. Her timing needed to be precise. Having lost some of her original force and momentum, Sally Lion Head swept her tail back across the crater rope. That was her mistake. At the exact moment that the tail crossed the rope, Molly landed on it, trapping it under her bare toes. With one swift movement, she swung the sharp end of the javarod with all her might.

"My tail! Nooo, please, it's just so fluffy!" screeched Lion Head, as she peered into the crater, watching her tail disappear into the darkness.

With her tail missing and one of her three legs battered, Sally was struggling, and the fight had gone out of her. In one final act of defiance, with great courage and sheer willpower, Sally began shaking her mane. Molly, moving at the speed of light, had to be fleet-footed and nimble, as she ducked, dived and performed death-defying acrobatics to dodge the darts and snakes that flew at her. Fighting for her life, Molly dodged the final dart. She was nicked twice already and was bleeding. The next problem to overcome was a snake that had attached itself to her hair and was trying its best to bite her.

She grabbed the snake's head and began to grapple with it. To and fro they battled, but Molly finally managed to untangle the snake from her hair and fling it straight into the crater. Sally was devastated; she had thrown everything at this small girl and Molly had still come out on top. Very nearly defeated, Sally Lion Head crept to the end of the round but everyone watching knew that the end was near.

Molly would take no pleasure in knocking Sally Lion Head off the rope. She was a beaten woman. She returned to the rope for the next round with a heavy heart. Seconds into the following round and it was over. Molly feigned an attack on Sally's battered leg and tail. Sally moved to block the attack and, as she did, Molly twisted and quickly spun round. Taking Sally by surprise, Molly smashed into the Lion Head's last good leg.

The battle was over; Sally toppled into the crater, crying, "Nooo, it can't be! I am so cute and fluffy. I can't lose!" as she disappeared into the darkness.

The crowd erupted with a huge roar that echoed across the lunar landscape. "Molly! M. O. L. L. Y! Molly!" they chanted.

Molly felt a huge surge of pride and her heart filled with joy. The sounds of the crowd thundered through her soul. She suddenly felt dizzy, and her mind spoke to her again. Well done, young Molly, it said. I will await you in the final. Molly wobbled on the rope, as though a ghost had swept through her body. Something or someone had vacated her mind, and her aches and bruises from the previous rounds suddenly came back in full force.

All of a sudden, Molly was acutely aware that the last few days had been very tough indeed. Luckily, she was already at the crater edge and able to stagger onto firm ground. Pod was on hand to grab his fragile friend and lead her back to their camp and a couple of hours of well-deserved rest.

CHAPTER TWENTY-ONE

The king sat back into his comfy throne, a large glass of moon vino in his hand. He was feeling very content indeed. His plans were coming together nicely. His best spy, one of many who had been reporting back to the king, had just been to him to report on the day's proceedings. Secretly, the king had been compiling a dossier on all the finalists. He was aware of Molly's success and knew of her popularity. He also knew about Carnaverous, and about Chunky's strengths and weaknesses. There was a file for every entrant somewhere in the pile before the king.

Sipping his wine, he smiled slyly. No one yet had a clue as to his plans. Even those closest to him continued to be of the belief that the games were a celebration of the king's reign and a chance to bring the people of the Moon together. The king couldn't wait until the final day of the tournament to reveal his plan. The time to reap the benefits of his plan were near which, most important of all, meant finally making the patterned planet pay.

*

CHAPTER TWENTY-TWO

After a sound sleep, Molly felt rested. She danced around the camp fire with Pod, Mank and even Ratabat. Using his skills of stealing alcohol from drunken men, Pod had gone up-market and stolen a bottle of Craterpagne, a very fine wine grown from a sweet fruit that grew just within the crevices of the lunar craters. Protected from the harsh moon winds, the berries grew large and unblemished. When fermented, they turned into a potent brew. Pod's latest victim probably wouldn't notice his missing bottle and would probably believe that he had drunk it himself.

The gang were celebrating Molly's semi-final win over Sally Lion Head. Molly was a little light-headed and it was a good thing that the final was not for a couple of days. Lively music drifted across the camp and Molly, determined to get some rhythm in his life, grabbed Pod and began to spin around and around with him, dancing with abandon. Faster and faster they spun, until eventually the pair landed in a tangled heap on the ground, giggling and laughing. At that moment, Molly was carefree, content and happy, blissfully unaware of the troubles ahead.

Pod, meanwhile, was wondering how he could finally kiss Molly, although he didn't have a clue how Molly would react and he completely lacked the courage to try. Telling himself to stop being so pathetic and man up, Pod was about to pucker up when Mank jumped straight on top of them. Molly erupted in laughter and the moment passed. Feeling despondent, Pod made his excuses and told Molly he was off to find some food. Molly, rolling around with Mank and Ratabat, never even noticed her friend walk off with his head bowed.

His mood getting bleaker by the minute, Pod kicked a discarded bottle at his feet, sending it flying through the air. He wandered aimlessly around the tournament site, not really knowing where he was going. After some time, he became aware that he was in a strange and new part of the site. This was the outsider quarter and the temporary home of the clans and teams from the far reaches of the Moon.

Pod's senses were assaulted by a strange heady blend of smells that were both intoxicating and quease-inducing. Ahead of him, around a camp fire, sat five cloaked men with shaved heads. The men's heads were covered in tattoos and they spoke in a foreign tongue. Between them, the strangers passed a long pipe, taking turns to inhale a strange-coloured vapour. They appeared to throw three small crocopig-shaped objects onto the ground with various outcomes depending on the shapes created when the objects landed. One of the outcomes involved downing an amber-coloured liquid.

Around the men, beautiful scantily clad women danced and poured drinks when required, sometimes feeding the men small morsels and exotic-looking fruit. They wore big baggy brightly coloured pants, their bellies exposed, and heavily jewelled tops with chains and gold adorning their necks.

Pod sat fascinated for a while, before he was spotted and the men jumped up, gesticulating wildly at him. Making a swift exit, he ran down a narrow passage. The men soon gave up and resumed their earlier and much happier pursuits. Pod, however, was completely lost. The alleys were dark and creepy, the moon fog was getting thicker by the minute, and strange noises startled him with every step he took. At first, he shook off the sounds, believing them to be rats and the usual night-time noises, but suddenly, a chill shot down his spine. He was sure he was being followed.

"Who's there?" he called out, but only silence answered him out of the darkness and mist.

A noise behind him made him turn swiftly but there was nothing there. Suddenly, as he turned back, something hard and heavy struck him on the back of his head. Staggering, he crumpled to his knees. Putting his hands to his head, he felt blood running through his fingers. As he fell to the floor, Pod could just make out the presence of someone bending over him before he drifted into unconsciousness.

Scarro bent down, cut a snippet of Pod's hair and, after a quick search of the prone Pod's pockets, removed a small trinket that belonged to Angel and the twins. Scarro grinned viciously – being in control of many of the gangs, he knew all of the goings-on and was acutely aware of Pod's father and how much Angel hated the boy. Angel would reward him generously when she discovered that Pod had been seriously harmed or worse in this lonely alley. Giving Pod a final kick to the body, Scarro set off in pursuit of his reward.

CHAPTER TWENTY-THREE

King Rufus stood on top of the winner's enclosure, running through his final speeches. Everything was at last in place; the enclosure exits could be shut in seconds, the king's own guard primed and poised. Every man knew what was expected of him; these were the king's finest men, ready and trusted by him. Satisfied that no more could be done, he retired to his quarters for the night.

Molly was blissfully unaware of the danger and predicament that Pod was in. After the physical toll of the last few days and having consumed a little too much Craterpagne, Molly was curled up fast asleep. The fire had died down; the embers flickered and danced to their own tune, looking like molten lava under the ash-covered charred and burnt logs. The noises of the camp had died down too, and Molly was relaxed and at peace. Suddenly, Mank jumped onto Molly's head and frantically began licking and pawing at her face.

Her dreams shattered, Molly struggled to open her

eyes as sleep refused to let her escape. Slowly she began to recognise her surroundings and her awareness returned. "What is it, Mank?" she whispered.

The cat turned round and round, meowing and scratching the floor, right where Pod should have been sleeping.

"Where's Pod?" cried Molly. "He's missing," she said, stating the obvious.

Although Pod and Molly weren't tied together and Pod frequently left of his own accord, he would never have left Molly out in the open, vulnerable and on her own for so long. She knew that if Mank was worried, Pod must have been missing for some time, and had not just nipped off to relieve himself or seek refreshments. Molly relit one of the half-burnt logs from the embers, and swung the makeshift torch around. The light danced across the darkness but there was no sign of Pod. Mank, with his nose to the ground, began to paw at the dust. Molly lowered the torch and could just make out Pod's footprint in the light lunar dust. It was a start. She could now see the direction in which Pod had set out and swiftly set off in pursuit, with Mank leading the way. With some difficulty, Molly could see and follow Pod's fading tracks for a while; however, once they reached one of the main camp avenues, she was at a loss. Pod's footsteps merged with dozens of others. Clueless, she sat down, as dirt-stained tears ran down her cheeks.

"Where are you, Pod?" she uttered in desperation.

Slowly, she began to feel a wriggling in her breast pocket. It was Ratabat, seeking an escape from the safe confines. Lifting Ratty gently out of her pocket, she placed the small bat onto the floor. "Oh, Ratabat," she sobbed. "I know that you want to help. If only you could fly."

With that, Ratabat started to hop and jump, getting a little higher each time. Flapping its little wings with all its might, the tiny creature hovered a while, rose a little but then swiftly fell in a crumpled heap on the ground. Pausing for a while to dust itself down and taking some deep breaths, Ratabat righted itself and tried again.

Clapping her hands, Molly shouted encouragement. "Go on, Ratty. You can do it."

Ratabat furiously beat its wings up and down. Slowly, it began to rise into the air.

"That's it," shouted Molly. "Now, control your movements."

With this, a sudden gust of lunar wind caught in the wing membrane, sending the poor bat spiralling through the air. Tumbling and twisting, Ratabat spun this way and that.

"Control!" screamed Molly.

Gradually, the dizzy Ratabat began to right itself, its spinning slowed, and its focus became clear, even though Molly and the lunar surroundings looked upside down.

"Ratty, turn round," guffawed Molly. "You're upside down!"

With a steady flapping of one wing, Ratty righted itself. Amazed at its new abilities, the little creature hovered up and down and occasionally, when feeling brave, twisted and turned.

"Well done," encouraged Molly. "Please, now find Pod."

Although elated with its new-found skills, Ratabat slowly drifted to the ground, shaking with fear at the prospect of flying into new and dangerous territory. Flying close to Molly was comfortable; going further afield was definitely not.

Sensing the bat's trepidation and using an understanding beyond her years, Molly gathered poor Ratabat in her arms. "Pod helped rescue you. Now he needs you," she whispered.

This was not strictly true, as Pod had wanted to eat and kill the baby bat. However, as Molly continued to talk, she slowly felt the strength and courage return to Ratabat. "You can be the hero, Ratty. Do it for me and for your new family," she enthused, kissing her finger and pressing it onto the bat's tiny head.

Ratabat took a long, slow, deep breath, flapped its wings and rose into the air. It circled around Molly's head a couple of times and then set off into the night. Following roughly the direction of Pod's last known tracks, Ratabat ducked and dived through the dark and dusty camp avenues. Feeling a little more confident, the little bat began to enjoy the sensation, lifting into the night sky and then swooping rapidly down along the dusty surfaces. Keeping an eye out for Pod and not really concentrating on its surroundings, Ratabat was completely unaware that it was being stalked. A large dusk dowl was leisurely following Ratabat's progress. It was a fierce predator and Ratabat was in danger. The dowl was dusky brown with a mottled belly, perfectly camouflaged in the night sky. It was the ultimate killing machine; its beak was the size of a man's hand and could snap a man's arm if required. However, it was the creature's claws that were its most potent force. They were sharp enough to tear the tough hardened skin of a crocopig to shreds. The mere touch of these claws could result in a lost finger.

Suddenly, as if sensing the perfect opportunity, the dowl dived towards Ratty, its razor-sharp claws extended, ready to grab the bat. At great speed, the dowl swept closer and closer to Ratabat, who was almost certainly doomed. But just as the dowl was about to strike, some primeval instinct alerted Ratty to the danger and it quickly swerved, just in time. The dowl overshot its prey and flew further up the lane. Ratty was now out of control. It tumbled and twirled, spinning wildly, and slammed into the wall of a local moozer. Dazed and dizzy, the little bat slid down the wall to the floor.

By now, the dowl had recovered and was turning mid-flight, preparing for the next assault, determined to catch its prey this time. Luck, however, was finally with Ratabat, and the moozer proved its saviour. Ratty had landed by the back door of the hostelry, where the ground was littered with discarded ale and moonshine barrels. Quickly coming to its senses, Ratabat crawled through a small hole in one of the barrels. The dowl was enraged. It swept towards the barrel with the frightened bat inside and began aggressively attacking the barrel with its sharp and powerful claws, tearing off chunks of wood. But then the dowl made a serious error of judgement, one that saved Ratty and probably Pod too, who happened to be lying unconscious in an alley not far away. For reasons known only to the dowl, it now began to attack the barrel with its fearsome beak. Banging and pecking at Ratty's hiding place, it bashed at it with greater and greater force and determination. Surely the barrel couldn't resist this sustained battering for much longer. The dowl could sense that the prize was within its grasp and drew its head back for one final powerful lunge. The razor-sharp beak plunged deep into the wooden barrel and promptly became stuck. The dowl snorted in rage, as that was all it could do. Flapping its huge wings, it tried to escape its woody restraints but found itself well and truly stuck. It tried everything, hopping about and pulling, but its beak was going nowhere. Once Ratabat was sure that the dowl was stuck, it crept cautiously from the barrel. The very angry dowl could only look on in disbelief as cheeky Ratty performed a little dance and then gleefully lifted into the air and flew off into the night.

Realising how very lucky it had been, Ratabat swept along in delight. But now it had to concentrate on the task at hand. Valuable time had been lost and Pod remained in desperate need. Having now mastered the basics of flying, Ratty began to quickly sweep up and down the camp alleys. Suddenly, out the corner of its eye, Ratty spotted a dark lump slumped on the ground. Adjusting its flight, Ratty swept towards the mysterious mound. As it approached, a prone figure began to materialise out of the darkness. Relief flooded through the little bat. It was Pod.

The bat landed near the head of the poor boy, hopped

onto his chest and furiously began licking Pod's face with its rough little tongue. Desperately trying to revive Pod, Ratty jumped about, pulled the boy's hair, nipped and gently pecked at his face, doing all it could to get a reaction.

After some time, Pod gradually began to stir. Softly groaning, he flickered an eye open, and weakly lifted his arm to gently stroke Ratabat. Reassured and feeling a little more confident that Pod might make it, at least for the time being, Ratty knew that it had to find Molly and quickly. Giving the unfortunate Pod one final lick and nip, Ratabat rose slowly into the air. Fluttering up and down above Pod's head, Ratty tried its best to tell the boy not to worry and that help would soon arrive. Pod nodded slowly and waved Ratty off. Happy that Pod had understood, Ratabat zoomed back in Molly's direction. Quickly dodging up and down lanes, Ratty flew past the still trapped dowl, who had managed to lift the barrel and was now shaking its head and bashing the barrel onto the floor.

Molly was now back at the camp fire; she stoked the dying embers into a roaring flame. She hoped that the fire would act as a beacon for the lost bat; she was right. Ratabat flew as fast as it could towards the bright flames. It burst into the clearing, breathing hard and, nearly exhausted, landed on Molly's outstretched hand.

"Oh, Ratty," cried Molly. "Did you find Pod?"

Ratabat jumped up and down on Molly's palm.

"Well done," Molly said as she took the movement to

mean yes. "Is he okay?" Molly asked urgently.

Slightly slower, Ratty again jumped up and down.

"I know that you are tired," she said, "but please, I need one last big effort from you. Let's go and find Pod."

Ratabat flew off Molly's palm, circled a couple of times to regain its bearings and then shot off, with Molly following swiftly behind. Quickly and without incident – the dowl had disappeared – they made it to the still prone Pod. Molly rushed up to her stricken friend, knelt down and cradled his head in her arms. Tears fell from her face onto Pod's and this stirred him a little. His eyes fluttered open and he smiled weakly at Molly and then squeezed her hand.

"It's okay," she whispered. "You're going to be okay and I will get you help."

With this, Molly picked up a stick and began beating anything that she could see, all the time howling and screaming, "Help! Help!" She made a massive commotion and generally tried to be as noisy as possible. Lights began to appear in the camps around and heads began to poke out from tents. The guards had raised the alarm. Molly had done enough. Leaning down, she gave Pod a quick kiss and turned to leave.

Pod grabbed her wrist, pulled her close and whispered in her ear, "Now go and win it for me!"

"Well, you get better for me!" she replied before stepping back into the shadows just as the first of the king's guards rushed around the corner. With the exhausted Ratty sound asleep in her top pocket, Molly didn't want to cause a fuss and didn't want the guards to ask her any difficult questions. She stayed just long enough to watch the guards tend to Pod and then stretcher him off to the nearest field casualty tent.

Wearily, Molly trudged back to her camp. What a night, she sighed. Once back at camp, she quickly fell into a deep sleep.

CHAPTER TWENTY-FOUR

As the bright orb of flames finally began to escape the confines of the darkened patterned planet, rays of brilliant light swept across the camps and the entire landscape of the lunar world. Chasing away the darkness, another day dawned. It was going to be warm and Molly was already stirring. Opening her eyes slowly, she stretched herself fully awake. Her face was etched with worry for Pod. Jumping up, she made sure that Ratabat and Mank were fed and watered before she set off to find Pod and check his condition.

Finding him, however, proved difficult, as Molly had no idea to which medical centre the guards had taken him. It took several hours and a fair amount of talking to sleepy people before Molly finally found the field hospital where Pod was being kept under observation. Luckily for Pod, one of his rescuers was a captain of the guard who knew the boy's connections. Pod's father had been informed and had then pulled some strings. The boy was in a modest, up-to-date and spotlessly clean establishment, which was a rarity for many of the makeshift clinics set up for the tournament.

The many different tribes and cultures liked to tend to their own, for treatments and aftercare, and as a result each area had its own field hospital.

Molly quickly made her way to Pod's bed. He was going to have to pay her back big time when he got better – she had bartered a couple of her finest trinkets to the old hospital cleaner for precise information of his whereabouts. However, when she rounded the corner and saw Pod's bandaged head for the first time she immediately forgot about her trinkets. He was deathly white and looked drawn and haggard. He had lost a lot of blood overnight and, although conscious, was still gravely ill. Molly rushed towards him and flung her arms around him.

"Hey," he cried. "Get off me. Anyone would think you cared!"

"Shut up," uttered Molly, tears streaming down her cheeks. "I thought I'd lost you. I was so worried."

"Don't be daft," whispered Pod, tired already. "It would take more than a tap on the head to stop me!"

It was clear to Molly that Pod was trying to be brave because, on uttering those words, he promptly collapsed back to the bed and fell asleep.

Molly adjusted his bedding and wiped his sweating brow. She then sat on a chair and rested her head on his bed. The next thing Molly knew, Pod was gently shaking her awake. The adventures and exploits of the last few days had obviously taken their toll.

"Molly," said Pod. "Quick! You must leave. I am not really allowed visitors at this time and I should be on bed-rest.

The doctors and nurses are on their way. I can hear them."

Shaking the sleep from her eyes, Molly jumped up.

Pod grabbed her arm and pulled her close. "Seriously, I will be fine. Win the competition for me. You can do it," he whispered. "Now, you must go quickly. Oh, and Molly, thank you for saving me."

"It was Ratabat who really saved you. The little bat was amazing!"

With this revelation, Molly scooted out of the ward and disappeared around the corner just as a white-clad doctor and three nurses filed into the room.

CHAPTER TWENTY-FIVE

Molly rushed back to her camp. Mank was still curled up asleep. "Don't worry, Mank," she said, playfully prodding him. "Pod is going to be okay, just in case you're concerned."

However, with Pod laid up, Molly would have to rely on Mank for support and she would need to train and prepare for the final by herself. There was a lot to be done and she had only one day left to get focused and ready. She would need to spend her time wisely. She wanted to make Pod proud and win the competition for him. She knew she would put the promised prizes to good use and even thought about extending Sate to accommodate Pod and her growing family. She had already made the decision that Pod would have to stay with her until he was fully recovered; there was no way the horrible Angel was going to get her grubby hands on him. She would get the truth out of Pod once this was all over. Molly was dying to know the connection between Pod, the large house, the twins and the disgusting Angel.

Molly's stomach suddenly rumbled, reminding her that

it had been several hours since she had last eaten. Mank, who had already had breakfast but was always hungry, looked at Molly expectantly as she picked up the Nitsplitter.

"Don't worry, Mank. I will get you some food and then I must practise. I have a big day tomorrow," sighed Molly.

The good thing about the tournament and the hordes of people watching and competing meant that there was no shortage of food. Molly returned to the camp within an hour, her arms laden with exotic delights. She had even managed to find a fresh moocean fish, big enough for the three of them. The city was miles from any moocean, so such a delicacy was rare. This particular fish just happened to fall off an overfilled wagon destined for the king's pre-final celebrations.

Molly, Mank and Ratabat had their own banquet, which was too late for lunch but too early for dinner. In keeping with her surroundings, Molly announced the feast a lunner and chuckled to herself, although her two companions just stared at her blankly.

Afterwards, feeling a little full, Molly dragged herself up and forced herself to start training. She was soon fully focused, however, and excited at the prospect of competing in the final. She really put herself through her paces. After several hours of hard physical effort and practising her moves, balance and stature, Molly decided that she was as ready as she would ever be. Her body was tuned to perfection and her mind, which was often filled with self-doubt and a lack of belief, was fully focused. She wanted to win; she had to win for Pod and for her friends.

The exercise regime had left Molly hot and sweaty, so she grabbed a towel and set off for the cold but refreshing showers under the falls.

It was evening when Molly returned feeling refreshed, happy, excited, nervous, scared, slightly sick and hyper all rolled into one big ball of anguish tight within her belly. Oh, how she wished Pod was here. He would know what to do and would offer wise words and encouragement. She stoked the camp fire embers, played with and tickled Mank and Ratabat, sang to them and told them stories and then tried her best to settle down.

Unfortunately, nothing she tried worked and, much as she loved them, Mank and Ratty were not the best conversationalists. Molly was restless and couldn't relax in her current state. It was then that she heard the sweet sounds of music drifting across the camps. Realising that sleep was intent on eluding her, she stood up and decided to follow the music. The sound of the music grew louder as she darted between the shadows, working her way towards the sounds. They were coming from the king's great hall.

Molly quickly darted behind a tree as she heard a guard approach. Luckily for her, the guard was preoccupied by a large lox roast roll that he was intent on eating as quickly as possible. Eating food on duty was frowned upon and the guard was trying his best to avoid a reprimand by stuffing his face full. Once Molly was sure that the danger had passed, she crept up to the wall of the huge barn-like hall.

The moon king's great hall was the oldest part of the castle. It had been in use for centuries as a venue for weddings, funerals, councils of war, as a hospital and as the main meeting place for all the moon people. The great hall had seen it all. The walls were crumbly, pockmarked and covered in mivy. This quick-growing plant covered huge areas of the walls, forever threatening to engulf the entire building. It certainly kept the king's gardeners busy. However, it also allowed Molly to easily climb up to the windowsill of a large ornate window. Once there, she sat and peered through the window.

The hall was packed with the king's friends and allies. Closest to the window, and to Molly, was the Earl of Loonshire, a huge man who enjoyed the king's hospitality a little too much. The earl laughed loudly. His battle tunic was stretched tightly across his rather large stomach and Molly held back a chuckle as she imagined the poor earl wearing the tunic into battle for real. He was surrounded by tough burly guards who ensured that the battle tunic had never been worn in anger.

Stretching across the hall, tables were strewn with representatives of all the nationalities of the Moon. The revellers were clearly having a good time. Plates were laden with food. Bottles, jugs, tankards and glasses were filled to various degrees or discarded wherever the drinkers fancied. Sprawled across one of the tables, an unruly mwarf snored loudly and a couple of his friends were now taking the opportunity to write rude mwarf words across his face. Luckily, no one else could read them. If they could, a war might have broken out there and then. Worse for the unfortunate mwarf, however, was that his friends were placing tiny coloured ribbons in his scruffy beard. He would not be a happy chappy in the morning.

In the centre of the hall, the same ladies that Pod had seen the previous evening were performing a sultry sexy dance. Judging by the rapturous roars and extravagant cheers that followed every sway and move, the crowd was clearly enjoying the spectacle.

At one end of the hall, three huge loxes were being slowly roasted over huge open fires. Slave boys sweated profusely as they tried to keep the loxes turning smoothly. The heat and smells only added to the intoxicating atmosphere and Molly seemed sure that the temperature was helping to keep the drinks flowing freely.

The largest and grandest table was at the opposite end of the hall to the fires where the temperature was much cooler. Here, the king and his closest family and friends sat. The people at this table were so laden with bejewelled necklaces, rings and crowns that they must have struggled to move. Diamonds, rubies, emeralds and all manner of jewels were on show. The party had really gone to town and they were decked out in all their finery. The entire table glittered and sparkled; any slight movement sent dazzling rays across the room.

The king appeared to be in serious conversation with his most trusted general. He seemed sober, intent and focused. The others at the table were behaving at least as bad as the rest of the great hall. An amorous young lord was paying a little too much attention to a beautiful young serving girl, or he was, until a swift whack around the head from his rather stern mother pulled him back in check.

Molly was transfixed. She could only dream of attending such a lustrous party and could almost taste and feel the food, drink and atmosphere. Suddenly, a vivid memory of a little girl flashed into Molly's mind. The girl was dressed as all princesses should be and even had a small crown perched upon her eloquently coiffed hair. Her dress was a delicate pink and had tiny lace bows decorating the hem and neckline. The little girl obviously loved the dress and twirled around and around so the dress billowed out. This memory then skipped forward: the little girl was being introduced to a huge party in this same great hall.

A huge roar and several loud crashes swiftly bought Molly back to the here and now and her position on the windowsill. She tried to cling to the memory but it was already disappearing back into the mists of her mind. Shaking her head clear, she focused her concentration again on what was happening in the hall. A raucous squabble had broken out. The guards were rushing to two individuals who appeared to have taken offence at each other and were now trading blows.

Molly had to rub her eyes; she couldn't believe what she was seeing. One of the fighters was Chunky. Molly couldn't believe it. How had the Moon Monkey got into the party? Chunky, at that moment, had one of the drunken mwarves in a tight headlock and was bashing the unfortunate fellow's head on the table. Three guards rushed to the mwarf's aid, one of whom Chunky sent sprawling across the table. Several more guards arrived on the scene to restrain Chunky. He continued to struggle and managed to knock one guard unconscious and gave another a bloody nose.

By now, twenty guards were on the scene, and not even the mighty Chunky (in his eyes, that is) could escape that many of the king's finest guards. Greatly outnumbered, Chunky was soon spreadeagled on the ground. Three guards pinned each arm and leg roughly to the ground. Chunky howled in rage and frustration. From outside the window, Molly could hear his expletives and threats.

Soon more guards arrived with chains and heavy locks and, after several attempts on the struggling Chunky, they finally secured and trussed him up like a celebratory lurkey murkey. The king, suddenly feeling extremely brave, walked up to Chunky and gave him a swift kick in the ribs.

"You fool," he spat in Chunky's face. "I had big plans for you. How do you think a disgusting specimen like yourself managed to get a seat at my table? Take him to the dungeons and sober him up. I need this imbecile," he ordered as he roughly shoved one of the guards.

He then stomped back to his table, pausing only to take a bottle of vino from a sleeping duke. His earlier jubilant mood was now sombre and he began to shout and order his servants and slaves about, swiftly whacking the young boy closest to him around the ears.

Molly was transfixed and also pleased that the horrible Chunky had got his comeuppance. However, she wished that she could teach the king some manners. He was rude and horrible to his staff and those he deemed beneath him which, in the king's mind, was everyone.

Molly's limbs were beginning to ache from perching on the small ledge. She tried to move her leg to relieve the pain but, to her surprise, her foot was stuck fast. The more she wriggled and twisted the tighter the grip on her ankle. Starting to panic, she adjusted her upper body and peered over the edge. The fast-growing mivy had curled and curved its way around her ankle. Now that she knew what the problem was, she wasn't so worried. She reached for the Nitsplitter, knowing it would make short work of the pesky plant.

Unfortunately, the mivy had other plans. As Molly moved her hand, super-fast tendrils shot around her wrist, securing it tightly. With surprising speed and catching Molly completely unawares, more tendrils spread rapidly around her other wrist and leg. The more she wriggled and struggled, the tighter her restraints became. Now she was in trouble, and it was she who was trussed like a lurkey murkey.

She opened her mouth to cry for help but as soon as she did so a green tendril shot across her mouth, effectively gagging her. Her cry for help was cut short and quickly descended to a whimper. Molly was in deep trouble. She knew unless she got help fast then all hope of the final was gone. Gradually, the binds became tighter, like a giant snake crushing its prey; her very life force was being sucked out. The mivy was applying great pressure to Molly's ribs and, as they began to creak, darkness encroached on her mind and she began to slip into unconsciousness. She only had seconds left and her breath was now shallow and laboured.

Out of the blue, Mank leapt onto the stricken Molly.

With his claws extended, he instinctively knew to cut the most dangerous restraints. He sliced and tore at the tight tendril around Molly's neck until she was free of it. Molly sucked a huge lungful of sweet moon air into her lungs which, by now, Mank had released from the tendrils constraining her ribs. Molly's strength quickly returned as Mank worked on releasing her arms. With one arm free, she could now release the Nitsplitter. A calm rage descended on her. The mivy was no match for the combined forces of the Nitsplitter and Mank's claws and teeth. Chopped, mashed, torn and shredded, bits of shoots and greenery flew into the air, landing on the ground like confetti and moon dust.

Having been chopped a little too vigorously, however, the mivy could no longer take Molly's and Mank's weight. Molly now found herself falling through the air. The ground approached rapidly and she landed heavily. The landing winded her and then Mank thudded down on top of her. She wrapped her arms around the stinky scruffy ragtag cat, kissed the creature hard and began to laugh, much to Mank's disgust. Molly's infectious laugh and outpouring of affection soon had Mank on his back waving his paws in the air and waiting for a tickle, as the pair rolled around on the ground, playing in the dirt and mivy cuttings.

They were both immensely pleased to have survived this most recent traumatic event but the noise they created alerted a nearby guard. With his sword raised, the guard rushed towards them. Molly heard his large boots crunch on the gravel just as he was about to charge around the corner. She quickly scooped Mank into her arms, threw the startled cat into the nearest hedge and dived in after him. Mank was about to protest when Molly stuffed her hand over his mouth. The guard was by now only inches from them and any small sound would surely have given away their makeshift hiding place.

Molly was sure that they would soon be discovered, even though their current good fortune seemed to be holding. The guard, however, was staring intently up at the window, the broken mivy and the dislodged dust on the window sill causing him some concern. Using his limited brain power, he concluded that someone had broken into the party. Worried that he would be in serious trouble with his superiors for letting someone sneak past on his watch, the guard rushed off to rally some support.

Molly needed no encouragement to scoop Mank up in her arms and set off at a run. She was eager to put some distance between them and the guard who was sure to return with more muscle and brain power.

Once Molly was sure that they were out of danger she slowed to a walk. "Far too much excitement for one night," she whispered to Mank. "It's time for bed. Believe it or not, we have a big day tomorrow."

The journey back to camp was uneventful and Molly and Mank were soon tucked up in bed. The patterned planet was high in the sky, its vibrant colours shining bright in the dark night. Molly offered a swift prayer to the gods and settled down to bed.

Across the tournament grounds, at the hospital, Pod was restless. He was determined to get to the final, for

Molly's sake. Peering out of the window, he made a promise to the patterned planet that he would not let Molly down. He would be there to see her compete.

By now, the king was in his giant bed, surrounded by charts and reports. He suddenly looked up and out the window. The bright, beautiful patterned planet was shining at him. The planet's vibrant colours were a constant insult to the king. He suddenly picked up his half-empty goblet of vino and threw it towards the window. Muttering insults, he clutched his plans and shouted, "Soon, it is happening. Not long now!"

Chunky was desperately trying to maintain his space on the only mattress on the jail floor. This was proving no mean feat and several skirmishes had already broken out. Chunky was having none of it and managed to prove that the bed was his, although others crammed onto any inch of space they could find. Desperate for sleep, Chunky had to stay alert to dodge the constantly flying legs and elbows. High in the jail wall, the patterned planet shone brightly through the very small barred window and onto the jail floor. The occupants hardly noticed it.

Carnaverous sat quietly in his rune-adorned tent, cross-legged and in a meditative state, chanting his mantras and preparing his body for the day to come. The master was feeling relaxed. The sudden appearance of the patterned planet filled the great man's mind.

Across the huge tournament fields, the noise subsided and the restless settled. Sleep was king now. Tomorrow would be finals day!

CHAPTER TWENTY-SIX

Pod was awake and alert before dawn. He had a plan afoot and he made a promise to himself to watch Molly in her final. During quiet times in the ward, Pod had been secretly exercising his legs, stretching and squatting. His head felt much better and his health was returning. He was confident that he could escape the confines of his bed and the ward. He needed a diversion and knew just how to create it.

Early in the morning, Pod was awoken by lively grunting and snorting. Judging by the racket being created, he suspected that the noise was coming from very close to his makeshift hospital bed. The occasional strong whiff of animal confirmed his suspicions – someone attending the games was keeping their animals tethered nearby. They were likely fattening the creatures up for the closing ceremony and, judging by the smell and noise, they were moon hogs, greedy little creatures that consumed everything in their path. They were kind of cute in their own way, with large bellies, tiny eyes and double snouts that could smell a morsel of food a moon mile away. Completing the funny look, moon hogs had not one but two curly little tails. Their presence was perfect for Pod's plan.

Pod slowly slid out of his bed, taking great care not to disturb the other patients. He had stolen a scalpel from the operating theatre the night before and now carefully removed the instrument from its hiding place. He used the surgeon-sharp scalpel to cut a small tear in the tarpaulin that formed the walls of the temporary hospital and crept through the gap. Once outside he inhaled deeply the fresh lunar air. Pod's eyes took a little while to adjust to the pre-dawn light, but the pungent smell helped. Sure enough, just a little way off, he could vaguely make out the outline of three moon hogs in the early morning mist. They were tethered to a pole on the edge of a makeshift camp. Already awake, they appeared to be scratching in the dirt looking for food.

Perfect, thought Pod and he slowly crept towards them, leaving a trail of food in his wake. Already, the sensitive snouts of the hogs had picked up the scent of the remnants of Pod's dinner leftovers and were straining at their leashes. It took a little effort on Pod's part and a quick flick of the razor-sharp scalpel to slice through their tethers.

Once free, the hungry hogs reared up on their hind legs, bellowed in satisfaction and immediately began to gobble up the scraps along the trail. They halted for only an instant at the hastily made tear in the hospital tent. The lure of the juicy pile of food that Pod had left just inside the tent was too much for the hogs to bear. One after the other they charged through the widening gap. Once inside, they were, quite possibly, as happy as pigs in muck. The bedside treats left by visiting friends and relatives were quickly consumed. Soon, the patients were screaming and shouting for help. Chaos and mayhem ensued. The hogs charged around, knocking over tables, chairs, charts and medicines.

The noise and madness drew doctors, nurses and guards to the scene. The influx of new people only added to the melee and the hogs, spooked by the noise and attention, began to charge at the newcomers. Soon, the hospital staff were being bowled over, legs and arms flailing in all directions.

Peering through the tear in the tent, Pod could only laugh at the chaotic scene. Perfect, he thought. Now he could make his escape and no one would be any the wiser.

CHAPTER TWENTY-SEVEN

At the same moment, on the other side of the city, the king held a jewel-encrusted handkerchief to his nose. Not at all happy with his surroundings, the king was about to give Chunky a big surprise. King Rufus had entered the dungeons. This was unheard of, and had the jailers and guards scurrying in all directions. Covered in mouldy crumbs and smelling of old cigarettes, the two jailers closest to the king jumped to attention, quickly brushing down their battered and foul-smelling uniforms, as they desperately tried to block the king's view, as others quickly cleared up the illegal card game that had so suddenly been interrupted. Even the rats had stopped gnawing, scavenging and doing all the other unsavoury things that rats do, their attention turned to the commotion.

The king's party, including his advisor and courtiers, were trying their best to make the king turn back, the disdain of finding themselves in such a disgusting place written all over their faces. The king, however, was determined see Chunky. When he was this determined nothing could stop him.

After a restless night, Chunky was finally snoring his

head off. Having fought for his pitch, he was now relatively comfortable in the knowledge that he had won the right to this piece of the crusty mattress. It came as some surprise then when a boot suddenly crashed into his back.

"Wake up, you oaf!"

Enraged, Chunky grabbed at the boot and was even more surprised when he felt the finest leather and a boot without a single hole. It seemed impossible in this location. Surprised, he looked up into the face of the boot's owner. Shocked beyond belief, Chunky thought he must be dreaming but was swiftly brought back to reality when two guards, rushing to defend the king, began to beat Chunky mercilessly.

"Stop!" demanded the king and at once the beating ceased.

Clearing his head and focusing his eyes, Chunky could only marvel at the sight before him. There stood the king and about ten of his party, while jailers and guards rushed around, kicking prisoners out of the way and desperately trying to tidy up. Their actions only made matters worse. Chunky couldn't resist smiling. He puffed out his chest and suddenly felt very important.

Mustering all the strength and gusto that he could, he confidently asked, "What do you want? Can't you see I am busy?"

His utter disregard for manners and royal etiquette swiftly led to another beating by the guards. This time the king left them to it for a while before shouting at them to stop. Wiser now, Chunky decided to keep his mouth shut. Two guards roughly grabbed him by the arms and hauled him to his feet. The king peered intently at Chunky before suddenly offering his hand for Chunky to kneel before and kiss.

Chunky hesitated at first, glared angrily at the king and then made a decision that probably saved his life and instantly elevated his standing in the eyes and plans of King Rufus. Kneeling in front of the king, Chunky raised his head, kissed the king's hand and pledged loyalty to king and country. Impressed, the king called for Chunky to be released immediately and asked that he be cleaned, made presentable and brought to the royal quarters.

"Now get me out of this hovel!" he screamed. "Oh, and heads will roll if you neglect your duties again. And that includes card playing!"

With that, the king turned and departed, leaving his party, the guards and jailers to scurry in his wake.

Slowly peace and normality returned to the dungeon, but with the absence of Chunky, who was now being hosed down in the stables.

It took some doing and much grumbling by both parties but finally Chunky was looking half presentable and ready to meet the king. Chunky, who never really got nervous, was now standing outside the huge ornate doors that led to the king's quarters, feeling as close to nervous as he had ever been. He had no idea what was happening and only half an hour ago he was looking forward to another dreadful day in the dungeon. But now he was about to meet the king. And he smelled strange – or clean to you and me. He wore a very tight ill-fitting suit, his hair was brushed for the first time in his life and he felt most uncomfortable.

Suddenly, the doors opened and Chunky was roughly pushed into the room by a burly guard. The room was lavishly and ornately decorated in gold and purple. Even Chunky could tell that everything in it was expensive. In the middle of the room stood a huge, elegant and imposing desk and behind the desk, looking a little lost, sat the king. He gestured for Chunky to approach and invited him to sit. Chunky duly did as he was told.

Once settled, the king stared at Chunky for an uncomfortably long time. Chunky was suddenly angry. He felt a fool and didn't like his new surroundings or clothes. He was a gutter fighter and wanted to get back to the games and his gang. Even the dungeon was more familiar than this. He leapt to his huge feet, knocking the heavy chair straight over as he did so, as if it was made of matchsticks. Then he banged his fists on the desk.

"Stop at once," commanded the king.

Shocked at the power in his voice, Chunky froze mid-bang.

"Sit back down now!" shouted the king.

Chunky surprised himself by quickly doing as he was told.

The king felt the shift in power. He had Chunky's attention now and it was time to grasp his opportunity. Wasting no more time, he stated his intentions – he wanted Chunky to become one of his trusted lieutenants. He wanted to know that if he authorised Chunky's release, he could count on the Moon Monkey, when it mattered most.

Finally, as a grand sweetener, he offered Chunky untold riches if he obeyed and if the king's plans succeeded. The king also promised Chunky that he could return to the tournament.

Chunky didn't understand most of what the king was ranting about but he knew that freedom was nearly his, he could claim his title in the games and with some riches thrown in, it would be no bad thing. Without thinking things through or worrying about the future, Chunky spat on his huge hand, grabbed the king's hand and vigorously shook it up and down. In Chunky's world, this was as good as a pact.

Taking all this as a good sign, the king wanted to push home his advantage. From a drawer in the huge desk, he produced a document that was already prepared and ready to sign. Chunky was not the brightest of creatures and he struggled to read even the simplest of words. He looked at the document blankly. The king patiently showed Chunky what was required of him and where to sign. Not waiting a minute more, Chunky scribbled something that might have been his name but more likely was merely an X. The king seemed happy that Chunky had just agreed to become one of his men.

"You are free to go for now, Chunky," said the king. "Oh, and before I forget, you had better win your final, or else!"

CHAPTER TWENTY-EIGHT

Mank lay across Molly's neck and Ratabat was scrunched up in her hair. The tiny bat drew comfort from being wrapped in Molly's hair and had taken to falling asleep on her head most nights. Molly spent ages each morning untangling and freeing herself from tiny claws and bat wings. As Molly started to stir and stretch, she slowly grew more alert. Energy and excitement about the day ahead started to replace her drowsiness, drawing her towards what might unfold. Her heart began to pound as adrenaline and fear began to course through her body, steadily bringing her to a heightened state of alertness. It was Finals Day!

Molly jumped up, sending Mank sprawling and Ratabat flapping, which hurt, as anyone who has ever had their hair pulled will testify. Just then, she spied something unusual propped against a half-burnt log. Someone had been in the camp during the night to deliver this object, but none of the trio had stirred and no one had heard a sound. Intrigued, Molly approached the strange parcel with caution, picked it up and gave it a shake. As she shook it, a note fell to the floor. Molly bent to pick it up.

The short handwritten note read, "Good luck Molly. Make us proud. Your friends couldn't have you looking like a vagrant on your big day."

Molly recognised the writing. It was the same scrawled writing as the notes that had been attached to the Rord and the Nitsplitter. Molly was excited now and quickly ripped open the brown packaging. Inside was an outfit of exquisite beauty. It was an exact copy of that worn by the unbelievable Amamoon fighting women. Made from the finest animal skin, it was extremely tough yet very flexible. It was silky smooth to the touch and Molly couldn't wait to try it on. Quickly shedding her nightclothes, Molly pulled the new outfit on. It slipped on with ease and fit like a glove; it was like a second skin. It slipped and slithered across Molly's skin and was incredibly comfortable. Someone had obviously tailored it to exactly Molly's size and it looked as if it was moulded to her body.

A shrill whistle suddenly penetrated the air. "My, you are looking fit," a voice cried.

Molly, mortified, grabbed up her nightclothes and held them tightly to her chest.

"You can't afford to be embarrassed," said the voice, getting closer. "You will be competing in front of thousands soon!"

Molly now recognised the voice. It was Pod. Dropping her clothes, she ran and leapt into his waiting arms. "Pod," Molly cried. "You're okay."

"I told you I wouldn't miss your big day," said Pod,

gently lowering Molly to the floor. "Now give me a twirl. Where did you get such an exquisite outfit?"

"I have no idea," said Molly. "It was by the fire when I awoke this morning."

"Well, you are stunning and your poor opponent will be dazzled by your beauty and poise," said Pod.

Blushing madly, Molly scurried off to her tent to change, before Pod got any more ideas.

"Time to get serious," said Pod when Molly re-emerged clothed in her more familiar rags. "But first, breakfast," he said. "I'm starving!" He promptly produced some rashers and a fresh loaf that he had swiped as he escaped the hospital.

Soon the contented quartet of Molly, Pod, Mank and Ratabat were munching on freshly cooked breakfast. After they had eaten and rested a while in happy silence, Pod dragged Molly up and forced her to exercise and practise. Molly faked resistance but she knew it was jolly good to have Pod back by her side, even though he probably should have stayed in hospital for at least a couple more days. However, she certainly wasn't going to complain and enjoyed being put through her paces. She felt happy and free and ready to take on the world. She had her three best friends by her side and, for the first time, Molly felt confident that she could win her final.

Chunky was also ready. His breakfast has been a grand feast courtesy of the king and he was now clothed in the finest battle gear available, especially for a being of his size. The cape that hung across his huge shoulders was in the king's colours and Chunky felt unstoppable. What a change in fortunes. He was raring to crack some heads.

The king was excited too. Today was the day that the greatest armed force ever assembled on the Moon would be formed, although few of its new recruits were aware of their inclusion yet.

The king was also confident that Chunky would win; his grand plans were finally coming to fruition. His generals were primed and ready; those that had initial reservations were soon convinced and persuaded. It was amazing what the threat of losing one's head could achieve.

Yes, indeed, the king was ready.

CHAPTER TWENTY-NINE

Loud bells tolled over the moonscape, ushering everyone to enter the arena. Finals day was about to be declared open. Molly was eager to be near the front. This was possibly the biggest day in moon history and one that the storytellers would talk about for years to come. She didn't want to miss a single thing and she wanted to pull Pod closer to the action. Mank was having a good time weaving between people's legs, making the leg owners scratch and holler and direct kicks at the cat. It was working wonders as the annoyed people were dropping all manners of things and Mank made a killing on food and money.

Suddenly, a fanfare broke across the general cacophony of noise. Slowly and reluctantly, a hush broke across the gathering masses. The king appeared on the raised stand, looking resplendent in his finest state clothes. He positively sparkled from all the paraphernalia he wore and even those in the furthest reaches of the arena could see their king shimmering in the distance.

He declared the games a success and endorsed the virtues

of sportsmanship and fair play. He called the tournament a friendly event that brought different communities, races and religions together. He said the time was fast approaching when the inhabitants of the Moon would need to stand together and unite, ready to repel unseen forces of evil. Many of those in attendance didn't understand what the king was talking about but they cheered enthusiastically anyway.

Suddenly, King Rufus raised his arms and called for silence. With a huge flourish and great gesticulations, he announced the start of the finals parade, which would give all contestants the opportunity to wave farewell to their families, friends and the spectators in general.

Molly had just taken a sip of moonbeam juice. When she heard this part of the king's speech, she spurted the contents of her mouth all over the unfortunate Pod.

"What?" Molly exclaimed.

Recovering quickly from his sudden drenching, Pod decided to point out the obvious. "I think that you should be in that, Molly."

Molly was not listening. She was already darting in and out among people, pushing them roughly out of the way, carving a trail between the hordes, leaving them gesticulating and swearing behind her. As she progressed, she could see the contestants gathering in their respective fields of combat. Molly was nearly there but would first have to dodge through a line of guards that were protecting the route of the procession. To Molly, that would be a breeze. She was going to make it and she felt a huge grin spread across her face. It was finals day, and the culmination of all of her hard work and the pain and bruises she had endured made her feel immensely proud of what she had achieved so far.

Suddenly, a giant hairy foot was stuck in her way. It was Hunky, Chunky's second in command. Molly couldn't avoid the giant foot and was sent sprawling head over heels, landing head first in the moon dust.

Hunky laughed loudly. "Going somewhere, little one?" he rasped. "Well, you were!"

Hunky advanced on the stricken Molly, who was slowly recovering from her fall. A little grazed around the knees and looking like she had been dragged through a hedge backwards, Molly was a little shaken but generally okay. Hunky, with real menace on his face, was looking to change that. With snarling teeth, he flexed his big arms and reached out to grab Molly by the neck. But at that very moment, a huge bolt of powerful blue energy struck Hunky flush in the chest. The big Moon Monkey had no idea what had hit him, but he knew it hurt. The orb of energy knocked him clean off his huge feet, sending him sprawling into the watching crowd, knocking many of them over as well. Molly could only watch in wonder as she gingerly tried to get to her feet. However, she found that she couldn't move. She would later describe it as like being caught in a net. She was trapped in a bubble that completely encircled her body. She punched, kicked and struggled, but the bubble responded and moved to each of her moves or wriggles.

She couldn't understand what was happening and fell to her knees. To her surprise, she discovered that she was no longer on the ground. The bubble had risen into the air and there was daylight between Molly's knees and the lunar surface. She began to stamp on the base of the bubble but it flexed with each lunge. Next, she released the Nitsplitter and tried to stab through the bubble. The razor-sharp dagger slipped easily through the bubble, like a knife through butter, but as soon as she pulled the Nitsplitter back, the bubble resealed. There was nothing for it; Molly would have to see what the strange bubble wanted of her. She was now rising further upwards and was soon floating above the crowds.

People strained their necks and pointed at the strange sight of an unruly girl floating above them in a strange translucent bubble. One of the crowd recognised Molly and a hushed whisper spread across the arena. It was the brave little girl, who had won the hearts of the locals with her extraordinary crater walking skills. She was now floating over the guards, who could only look on in wonder at what was going on. They were powerless to stop Molly, not that they wanted to, and a few even began to cheer and wave their lances and swords in her general direction.

Unbelievably, the bubble was taking her towards her event meeting place and the other competitors. There was Christos, the young farmer boy, and of course Sally Lion Head, and other contestants in various states of well-being; some had broken limbs, others were being pushed in wheelchairs. Molly floated over all of them. Some even looked up and waved.

Now the bubble was descending. Molly couldn't believe

it; she was about to land right next to Carnaverous. As soon as the bubble landed by the great man's side, it disappeared.

"Hello Molly," said Carnaverous. "I couldn't let you miss the opportunity of beating Carnaverous the Great in the final!" he chuckled.

Molly, who had been following the other contestants closely, already knew that her final opponent would be Carnaverous the Great. Although, she never believed that she would get to speak to him beforehand; Carnaverous was known to be a recluse. Her legs, already grazed and bruised, nearly gave way completely.

Carnaverous offered Molly his arm as she tried to steady herself. "Now, now," he whispered. "People are watching. Don't go making a fool of yourself."

CHAPTER THIRTY

Regaining her composure, Molly glanced around. Carnaverous was right. Huge crowds surged towards them; the linked arms of the guards struggled to contain them. Everywhere she looked Molly could see heads of every shape, colour and size peering back at her. Expectation and joy were etched on all the faces. This was the biggest occasion that many had ever seen and they were intent on enjoying the day. Stories of the day would be recounted for generations to come and no one wanted to miss a moment of it.

A trumpet suddenly called the assembled masses to order, the band started to play the national anthem and the finest singers on the Moon began to sing. At long last, finals day was underway. The first event of the day was sword fighting. This was usually performed by armour-wearing knights and lords. It was deemed fitting that the nobility and the wealthy should lead the way for the procession, so these knights, gleaming in their shiny armour, led the contestants around the arena.

One of the knights was the seven-foot-tall Earl of Mare Frigoris. He cut a very imposing figure clad in his gleaming gold *Fleur de Lys* armour. It was rumoured that no other knight could even lift the suit, let alone wear it to battle. The earl's standard-bearer was dwarfed beside him but nonetheless waved the flag of Frigoris with great enthusiasm. This rather annoyed the knight as the flag continually flapped in his face.

Molly felt extremely sorry for the nervous-looking knight who walked next to the giant; he was surely in for a beating. But sometimes size didn't matter, or so Molly hoped as she cut a sly look at the imposing Carnaverous. The archers were next and, while not as imposing as the knights, Molly knew they were just as deadly. She vaguely knew one of the finalists, Bobbin Good, and had once seen Bobbin shoot three moonster bats with just one arrow.

Speaking of moonsters, Ratabat suddenly poked its head out of Molly's top pocket. The baby bat, slightly scared of all the banging and commotion, finally felt brave enough to make an appearance. Molly gave Ratty a kiss and placed it on her shoulder. Now Mank darted between a guard's legs and rushed to her side, leapt into her arms and began licking her face. Pod waved madly from the front of the crowd. Molly's family was complete and her heart surged with pride and happiness.

The hand-to-hand combat fighters were next in line and then it was Molly's turn! She could see Chunky at the head of his group and she definitely heard his battle roar. As the combat fighters moved off, Carnaverous grabbed her arm.

"Are you not forgetting something?" he asked, slowly looking Molly up and down. "I can't be seen fighting a waif."

Molly became acutely aware of her tattered and torn attire. In her haste to join the ceremony, she had forgotten to change back into her new fighting outfit. Glowing red with embarrassment, she was, for the first time, ashamed of her appearance. Wishing that the ground would eat her up, she wanted to run back to the safety of the Sate.

"I can't do this," she uttered. "People will just laugh at me."

"Molly," whispered Carnaverous. "You are special and talented no matter what you wear. Look at your friends. They love you for being you, not for money or fancy customs."

Molly slowly lifted her head and looked into the faces of Pod, Mank and Ratty. They all beamed back. In different ways, they all expressed love and pride, and Molly began to feel herself grow taller. Her earlier fleeting concerns were quickly washed away. She was Molly and didn't give a damn what she looked like. She would still give Carnaverous a run for his money.

The great man began to smile. He could see the transformation wash over Molly. Now she was ready. "However," he said, "I still can't be seen fighting a tramp. What if you win? Oh, the shame."

Laughing to himself, he removed his rune-covered cape and quickly covered Molly, Mank and Ratty. Uttering an incantation in a strange language, he waved his hands intricately, moving them faster and faster, until his fingers were a blur. Swiftly and majestically, Carnaverous removed the cape. Pod roared his approval. The transformation was amazing. Molly looked stunning. Her hair had been styled in the latest fashion and she wore make-up that would make the ladies of the court swoon in jealousy. Incredibly, she was also now dressed in the Amamoon outfit. If that wasn't good enough, Carnaverous had added the finest pair of knee-high fighting boots that money could buy, complete with touch-sensitive soles that would literally wrap around the crater rope. She looked sensational. She beamed from ear to ear and buzzed with excitement.

It was then that she noticed Mank or, at least, something that resembled Mank. Carnaverous had worked his strange magic on the scrawny scruffy cat. Mank was now spotlessly clean and his black fur positively sparkled in the moonbeams. The cat, however, was not happy and began to chase his tail, which had fluffed right up. Mank refused to believe that it belonged to him. Even Ratabat had been scrubbed up and was currently wearing a tiny tuxedo and a little bow-tie. Molly clapped her hands in joy and danced a little jig, spinning wildly around, her long clean hair flowing behind her.

"Now," boomed Carnaverous, "we are ready!" and held out his arm.

The mismatched small group set off with the other crater contestants.

The crowds roared and cheered, waved flags and shouted the names of their favourites as the finalists paraded around the arena. Molly's chest puffed with pride when she heard her name being roared more than once. The people had taken Molly to their hearts; she was already their champion. Mank walked with a spring in his step as he imagined he was a fearsome cave lion from the mountains of Huygens. Even Ratabat excitedly hopped up and down on Molly's shoulder.

Eventually, all the finalists arrived once more in front of the king. For once in his life, King Rufus was straight and to the point, for even he was eager for things to get underway. He raised his arm, dropped his jewel-encrusted handkerchief to the ground and declared in his most regal voice, "Let the finals begin!"

The contestants quickly scurried to their respective positions and those already eliminated joined the crowds of spectators, eager to see how the day would unfold. Molly, with a little time to kill before her event, decided to watch the first action of the day. However, it would seem that everyone else had the same idea, for when Molly approached the sword fighting arena, the crowds were already twelve deep.

Suddenly, Pod appeared by her side. "Come with me," he said. "I know just the spot."

He led Molly behind some food tents (Molly took great care not to get messy), then they scrambled atop a pile of old boxes and containers. They were now above the heads of the crowd and had the perfect view.

The Earl of Mare Frigoris was already warming up, swinging his huge sword in great sweeps above his head.

The smaller knight opposite still looked nervous but Molly could tell he was agile and quick on his feet and this could be to his advantage. The referee called the two together and asked for a good clean contest. Both men agreed, shook hands and retired to their corners, where they were handed their weapons of choice by their men at arms. It took two strong lads to hand the earl his chosen sword. Molly had never seen a weapon so big and surely no one could survive a hit from it.

An ear-splitting, deafening noise penetrated the atmosphere. The crowd roared with delight as the klaxon sounded for the first final of the day. The giant earl advanced towards the small, and still slightly shaking, young knight. The earl swung his sword menacingly. It looked to Molly as if the contest would be over before the excitement could begin. The crowd gasped collectively as he thrust the sword towards his opponent. Surely the blow would end the contest there and then. It certainly would have if it had connected, but the thrusting sword only hit fresh air.

With lightning speed, the young knight dodged the blow, spun around, rolled and landed a blow to the back of the giant earl's head, all in one fluid movement. Molly thought that she was quick, but the speed of the young knight was unbelievable. The earl stumbled to his knees, shocked and confused. The blow had hurt, but his pride had been damaged even more. Quickly getting back to his feet, he turned to face his rival once more. Again, he charged, swinging madly, only for the outcome to be repeated.

This time, the earl came out of it bleeding badly from

a wound to the back of his head. Feeling a little dazed and unsteady on his feet, he turned to face the young knight once again as the klaxon sounded for the end of the first round. Staggering back to his corner, the Earl of Mare Frigoris was relieved to have this welcome break. The crowd roared their approval. The first round had definitely gone to the young knight and the crowd loved the underdog.

The second round continued in the same fashion, with the young knight slowly but surely gaining the upper hand as the earl tired. Rounds three and four continued in the same vein. However, in the fifth round, the tide suddenly changed. The Earl of Mare Frigoris was a seasoned campaigner and he was not about to go down without a fight. Quietly summoning his last ounces of strength, he was ready for the young knight's next dodge. Believing the earl to be nearly defeated, the young knight's inexperience cost him dearly.

Rather telegraphing his next move, the young knight found himself flying across the heads of the crowd, the look of surprise on his face masking the pain he was feeling. The earl had faked an attack and then quickly reverse swung his huge blade, catching the poor knight flush in his midriff with the side of the great sword.

As the young man flew into the spectators, he knew the contest was over. The Earl of Mare Frigoris was declared the victor, the first event of the day was over and the crowd was in raptures. The fight had been good and the ending dramatic; the day had started well and the excitement was palpable.

CHAPTER THIRTY-ONE

Molly had enjoyed the fight and adrenaline was coursing through her veins. Soon, her own final would begin and it was time to prepare and warm up. The action was coming thick and fast, the events unfolding rapidly as the morning wore on. The archery had thrown up a surprise; the victor was a complete stranger from the dark side of the Moon, who had narrowly beaten Bobbin Good in a sudden-death arrow shoot-out.

Molly was distracted from her training and meditation when a massive roar went up. Chunky had entered the arena. He looked resplendent in the king's colours. Huge and muscular, he cut an imposing figure as he beat his massive fists on his chest and roared his defiance at everyone. Molly knew that with Chunky in this frame of mind, his opponent was in for a torrid time.

Chunky's opponent was on the other side of the arena looking completely unperturbed. Molly's jaw dropped as she saw a creature that she had always thought was merely a myth. It was a shape-shifter, currently in the form of a werewolf, nonchalantly licking its claws clean. Perhaps Chunky was in for a battle after all!

King Rufus watched on with intense interest. He had taken a huge leap of faith in choosing Chunky. He knew that Chunky was incredible strong and because of his low intellect, perfectly manageable. The Moon Monkey was just what King Rufus required. Scarro, the gangland boss, had been keeping the king updated on the Moon Monkey's work. He needed Chunky to win and had big plans for him. However, the shape-shifter would not be an easy opponent; his semi-final opponent had died after the contest. The king and his aides were keen to keep this fact quiet; the publicity would not be good.

The king really needn't have worried. With Chunky in this mood, a whole army of shape-shifters couldn't have defeated him. The early rounds were fairly even, with the two muscular fighters trading blow for blow. Chunky had a scare in round four when the werewolf plunged his claws straight into his shoulder. This move wasn't strictly within the rules, but the fight was getting ugly. Chunky didn't seem to notice the pain, although his shoulder was bleeding profusely and he must have been in pain.

The rounds continued and the battle was like two moon mountains clashing together; neither fighter gave an inch. As the blows continued to rain from one and then the other, Chunky fell to his knees but quickly recovered and came storming back. The shape-shifter was also bleeding from a variety of wounds and the fighting continued, fierce and intense. Both parties were beginning to tire and the effort of maintaining the werewolf form was proving increasingly difficult for the shape-shifter. It took great energy and concentration for the shape-shifters to maintain any one form. The werewolf was beginning to weaken. Slowly but surely, one huge hairy muscular arm with deadly claws began to change. Chunky spotted the weakness and pounced like lightning, striking the weakened human-like arm with immense strength. The shape-shifter howled in pain; his weakened arm clearly broken. Although hurt, he was not yet beaten. He lashed at Chunky with his strong arm. His sharp claws raked across Chunky's chest, ripping into the Moon Monkey's flesh like a hot knife through butter.

Reeling, Chunky staggered back, but the attack had cost the shape-shifter. His form began to hover in and out, one minute a fearsome brute of a beast, the next a slow-moving moon sloth, easy pickings for the superior Chunky.

Chunky knew that the contest was over; it was just a question of timing. It was now that the nasty side of Chunky appeared. He began to toy with the unfortunate shape-shifter, moving swiftly out of the way when the werewolf threatened and then attacking when the creature was in its moon sloth state. The crowd began to boo and jeer when they realised that Chunky was drawing the contest out, hurting the shape-shifter but not doing enough to win, humiliating the beaten finalist. The king was forced to step in when the crowd began to throw things at the taunting victor. He declared the unpopular Chunky the winner and the contest was over.

Chunky, deaf to the crowd, was euphoric. He beat his chest and roared triumphantly. The king smiled his approval. He had chosen well; Chunky was all that was required and more. He had found a loyal strong subject who could be manipulated and bent to his command.

The crowd had quickly lost interest and was already dispersing. Chunky was having none of it. He continued to race around the arena, beating his chest and roaring. Suddenly, he decided that one of the spectators was not giving him the attention he deserved. He launched himself across the small fence that separated the crowd from the action and viciously attacked an unsuspecting onlooker. The guards were forced to jump in and pull Chunky off the man before he killed him. The crowd was not pleased and Chunky had to be quickly led to safety before a full-scale riot broke out.

The king wisely called for his band to bring the games to order with a quick rendition of a popular shanty. He then announced an early lunch. He hoped this would give everybody a chance to cool down.

Molly could not even think about lunch – it was her turn next. Her meeting with Carnaverous was rapidly approaching and she was like a cat on a hot tin roof. She couldn't keep still as excitement coursed through her veins. This was her chance and only one person stood between her and glory. It was a shame that that person was the great Carnaverous. Pod tried his best to keep Molly's feet on the ground by offering advice and pearls of wisdom. Some of it even sank in!

King Rufus was really rather enjoying his lunch. The games had so far been a roaring success; the cream of the contestants had risen to the top. Chunky was perfect for his role and the final parts of the king's puzzle were falling into place. His plans couldn't be working better and Rufus sat enjoying fine food and Craterpagne with a rather smug smile on his face.

The final day of the championship was very nearly over and the next stage of the king's master plan was all set and ready to go.

CHAPTER THIRTY-TWO

Molly, completely unaware of what lay ahead, positively gleamed in her new fighting outfit and make-up; she looked beautiful. She was as ready as she ever would be and was chomping at the bit to get the contest underway. Mank, Pod and Ratabat had all helped and encouraged in their own individual ways. Pod hugged her and offered his pearls of wisdom; Mank purred encouragement and wrapped himself around her legs; Ratabat flapped and hovered in front of her face, then landed squarely on her newly washed, brushed and shaped hair, immediately tussling it up. To Ratabat, this made Molly look like Molly again.

Laughing, she mildly told Ratabat off. "You didn't like my hair then?" she teased.

Pod was pleased. The light-hearted banter had calmed Molly down and he could finally say that she was ready. "Bring on the old man Carnaverous!" he screamed.

At that instant, the klaxon sounded, declaring lunch over and the commencement of the afternoon session of the finals. Molly's interminable wait was finally over.

King Rufus returned to his throne, briefly called order and announced the names of the next two contestants. Molly felt a lump in her throat as the king said her name and hairs rose on the back of her neck as the king's voice sounded strangely familiar to her. However, she quickly dismissed the idea. Apart from the mysterious meeting that she had secretly observed in the palace gardens, she had never even met the king.

Right now, she had other more important matters to focus on. As if in a dream, she entered the crater arena. Taking her position on the edge of the crater, she took the opportunity to look at her opponent, Carnaverous the Great. He looked huge and resplendent in his cloak covered in runes and archaic symbols. To Molly, a shimmering halo seemed to surround him and a powerful aura was being emitted towards her. She felt her knees buckle before the fighting had even begun and she felt dizzy and bewildered. Luckily, Pod saw the strange effect that Carnaverous was having on her and rushed to her side. Pulling her swiftly away, he broke her stare and whatever hypnotic hold Carnaverous had gained over her.

Shaking her, Pod urged her to concentrate and focus. Slowly, Molly began to regain control, and her senses returned to their heightened state. Breathing deeply, she cleared the fog that surrounded her mind and pulled herself back to battle readiness.

"You must be strong," shouted Pod. "In body and mind! Stay focused and block him out. Concentrate only on winning. Be strong."

These were wise words and Molly knew that Pod was right. She felt invigorated, ready and more determined than ever.

Just in time, really, for at that moment, the klaxon sounded. Molly's final had well and truly begun.

CHAPTER THIRTY-THREE

The king had taken his seat and was intrigued. Carnaverous would be perfect for his plans although he would be very hard to control, if at all. Molly, on the other hand, was a mystery. He had seen the reports and heard the rumours and the crowd had taken her to their hearts. He knew that she must be a little special or she wouldn't have made it to the final. It was going to be an interesting battle.

Molly stood at the edge of the moon crater, the largest crater used so far in the finals. A gold rope, pulled taut, stretched across the gap and shimmered brightly in the glistening moonlight. Molly took her first step onto the rope, swaying slightly as her lithe body adjusted her balance. She felt calm and her body instantly became one with the rope. Every small movement, bounce and sway of the taut rope was compensated with subtle changes in Molly's stance.

She bounced suddenly on the rope, leapt into the air, completed a swift somersault and landed deftly back on the rope. The crowd cheered, immediately impressed by

Molly's skill and expertise. For the final, the contestants were allowed to choose their own weapon and Molly had chosen the javarod. Now she began to spin it. Faster and faster the rod spun until it became a blur. Then Molly began to advance along the rope towards Carnaverous. The great man was casually ambling towards Molly, waving to the crowd and grinning like a Cheshire cat. He looked as if he was about to embark on a casual afternoon stroll rather than a deadly fight with a dangerous opponent.

Molly was incensed. How dare he pay her so little respect. She rushed along the rope, the javarod spinning so fast that the air around it fizzled and crackled with static electricity. She crashed into Carnaverous, wildly swinging the rod at her opponent. The attack was rash and Carnaverous gave Molly a big shove with his weapon across her chest. She staggered backwards, out of balance and out of control, swaying one way and then the other. One of her feet slipped off the rope and she teetered on the edge of the abyss. But she was determined that she would not let the contest end before it had really begun. She breathed deeply, tried to grab back a little control and then leapt backwards into the air and somersaulted. She executed this move just in time, as Carnaverous smashed his rod straight into where Molly had just been standing.

Landing squarely back on the gold rope, she now felt more composed as she advanced once more towards her opponent. She feigned an attack with the javarod and then, with her left foot, deftly kicked the surprised Carnaverous directly in the head. Her opponent was rocked; it was the first time in the competition that a blow had been landed on him. He was more than a little dazed and shaky and quickly had to move back out of the way of Molly's next attack.

Molly had gained the upper hand in this round and Carnaverous spent the rest of it dodging her blows and attacks. She whirred, twisted and spun. Her attacks were lightning-like, swift and deadly, one second attacking the head and the next the legs. The javarod probed and slashed, Molly kicked and punched, displaying the full range of her undoubted skill. The highlight of the round was when she launched a huge leap, landing with one foot on Carnaverous's head. Using his head as a stepping stone, she then landed on the rope behind her opponent. Twisting sharply, she landed two blows to his back before he even realised what she had done.

Any normal opponent would have been obliterated, but Carnaverous was no ordinary opponent. However, he was relieved to hear the klaxon sounding to end the round. He left the crater more than a little out of breath. Molly's blows had found their mark and Carnaverous was hurt and somewhat shook up.

Molly was disappointed that the round had seemed to end so suddenly but, as she moved back towards Pod and firm ground, she realised how much effort and energy she had used. She practically fell into Pod's arms and gratefully gulped at the refreshing drink he offered her. Pod encouraged Molly, telling her how well she was doing and that she would win. Molly then looked across to see how her opponent was bearing up; she knew he must have been hurt.

She was, however, shocked. Carnaverous appeared completely recovered and relaxed, sitting on the ground with his eyes closed, chanting ancient incantations. Noticing where Molly was looking, Pod quickly turned his friend around to face him. Hoping that there would be no repeat of the beginning of the contest, he slapped Molly on the face.

"Ignore him," Pod urged. "You had him beat that last round. You must have hurt him."

Molly was incredible in the second round. Her movements were a blur and more than a few blows landed squarely on Carnaverous. She did not escape unscathed, however. One assault left her vulnerable and Carnaverous launched a deadly counter-attack. The great man's javarod caught Molly in the face and her nose exploded, causing blood to stream down her face. She feared that it was broken but didn't have time to worry about such matters now; she was fighting for her survival.

This time it was Molly who was relieved when the klaxon sounded the end of the round. Breathing heavily and beginning to tire, she trudged back to Pod.

Pod rushed to her, sat her down and began to stop the blood flowing from her nose. He carefully looked at Molly's nose and was relieved to see that it was not broken; it looked far worse than it was. He informed Molly of his verdict and urged her to finish the job. Again, Molly threw a quick glance in the direction of Carnaverous. Once again, he sat, relaxed and chanting, and didn't even appear to be out of breath. How was she going to beat this man?

Round three was soon underway. Almost immediately, Molly became aware that something had changed. Carnaverous seemed to hover above the gold rope, his feet barely touching the surface. His movements had become more gracious and sleeker, and he shimmered in the moonlight. The great man's rod seemed at one with his body, every muscle flowed with a surreal quality and he looked almost liquid.

Gritting her teeth, Molly advanced towards the shining apparition, spinning her own javarod unnaturally fast. Quick as a flash, she lashed out with her weapon, and the javarod sliced through Carnaverous's arm. It should have been a deadly blow, breaking her opponent's arm at the very least. But Molly leapt back in shock; her javarod had passed straight though her opponent's shimmering arm. Carnaverous was completely unharmed.

Molly, angry at such sorcery, moved forward again, intent on menace. This time she swung the javarod hard at Carnaverous's legs. She felt a little resistance when the rod first struck his leg but, as before, it passed straight through. Once again Carnaverous was unscathed and now it was Molly's turn to frantically defend as the great man launched his own attack.

She had to quickly retreat from the onslaught that she now faced. Molly had to use all of her skill and experience to dodge blow after frantic blow. Twisting, turning, leaping and spinning, she managed to avoid the worst of the attacks. The watching crowd could only hold their collective breath and "ooohh" and "aaahh" at the amazing display of fighting skill; nothing like it had ever been seen before – two masters of their trade competing at the height of their abilities.

Molly puffed hard. Her energy was being sapped and the exertion of the battle was beginning to take its toll. She dug deep in her reserves and, having just survived a brutal assault, launched into yet another attack of her own. Swinging the javarod with a power that few would have believed if they hadn't witnessed it, Molly flew at Carnaverous. The deadly end of the javarod swept towards her opponent's stomach. The contest was surely over now. No one could survive such an attack. Or so it seemed. Carnaverous stopped, stood upright and smiled. The javarod passed straight through his body, leaving him unruffled and unharmed. Molly was just cutting thin air; there was no resistance and she stumbled forward. Quick as lightning and just as deadly, Carnaverous brought his own weapon down on Molly's head, hard enough to cause a major headache but not enough to kill.

That was it. Molly's fight was over. She was falling and falling fast. Her feet lost contact with the gold shimmering rope and she disappeared into the abyss. Her arms and legs flayed in the air but no respite could be found. Bleeding from her head wound, she went crashing down into the crater. Spinning out of control, she hit the rescue netting hard, knocking the breath out of her body. The netting absorbed the power of the fall, she bounced a couple of times and then came to rest in the centre.

She didn't move. Her head was splitting and she was badly concussed. Her sight was blurred but at least she was alive. She breathed deeply, lay still and began to assess her injuries. She didn't think she could stand even if she wanted to; her legs were unsteady and wobbly. She was bleeding from several cuts. Her head wound was the worst and would need medical attention. Her body had been beaten black and blue and she ached all over. She took it to be a good sign that she could feel the pain. It meant she was still alive. It would take time, but she would heal. Safe in this knowledge, Molly closed her eyes, lay back and waited to be rescued. However, luck had deserted her. The safety net supporting ropes had been nearly sawn through; the last few fibres were now beginning to fray. Strand by strand, the threads stretched and snapped. Molly was heading towards disaster. If she fell into the crater depths there would be no return.

Suddenly, Ratabat was in Molly's face, flapping its tiny wings. Molly had fallen unconscious and the little bat now urgently tried to wake her up. This method had worked with Pod a few days earlier when he was in trouble and Ratty hoped it would work again. Molly slowly opened one eye and tried to swat the annoying bat away but Ratabat wouldn't give up.

Molly gradually became more aware of her surroundings. She opened both eyes and was immediately aware that she was in danger. Something was wrong. The safety net was listing badly to one side. She tried gingerly to stand but that was a mistake; the rope netting dropped a whole foot and began to wobble. Molly dropped to her knees and crouched utterly still, waiting for the rocking to ease. She knew she was in grave danger; the slightest wrong move would send her plummeting into the depths. Right now, her life was literally hanging by a thread.

In desperation, Ratabat had flown to the fraying ends, grabbed a few in its mouth and was urgently trying to hold them together. It was a brave but futile attempt; there was no way that poor Ratty could hold gravity at bay. As the loose ends began to slide through its jaw, tears welled in its small bat eyes. It was over. Ratabat had failed. The strained ropes gave one last creak and then two corners snapped. Molly fell and the situation grew even more critical. She was mere seconds from a grisly death; the rocks below would smash her tiny body to bits.

Ratabat's high-pitched mournful wail suddenly brought Molly back to her senses. This was not going to happen. She refused to contemplate that her death was imminent. Twisting quickly in the air, she released the Rord from around her stomach. Swiftly cracking the Rord like a whip, it shot out towards a stalagmite-like outcrop of rock and instantly wrapped around the spike. Molly was still falling and she prayed that the stalagmite would hold and that she wouldn't lose her grip on her magical Rord. Although the danger hadn't passed, the odds were now just a little more in her favour. Molly was still plunging into the darkness. Her fall felt like an eternity, when in reality it was seconds before the Rord snapped taut. When it did, Molly's arm was nearly ripped from her shoulder. She felt a tendon snap and howled in pain. Luckily, her recent training regime paid off and she managed to maintain her grip on the Rord. The stalagmite also appeared strong enough to hold her weight.

She was not out of danger yet. She felt dangerously weak, her head was splitting, her shoulder was in agony and every inch of her body growled with pain. She could feel herself slipping away; it would be so easy to close her eyes and rest. It was pitch-black inside the crater cavern as Molly dangled in the darkness, clinging as tightly as she could to the Rord.

Back on the surface, pandemonium had broken out. As victor, Carnaverous was supposed to meet the king and receive his trophy. The crowd was supposed to cheer and applaud, Molly was supposed to be presented as the gallant runner-up and another piece of the king's plan was supposed to have fallen into place. Instead, King Rufus was raging. Both contestants had completely disappeared. The king could just about manage Molly's fall to her death in the depths of the crater. After all, accidents do happen. The main cause of his anger was the victor, Carnaverous. As soon as Molly had lost her grip and fallen into the gaping crater, Carnaverous had bowed gracefully to the crowd and vanished in a puff of smoke and flames.

With no trace of either contestant, King Rufus was close to bursting. The crater walker was critical to his plans and to lose the best two on the Moon was a disaster. The crowd was turning hostile. They had taken the young girl from the Fogey's to their hearts and had made her one of their own. News of her death was not going down well.

To make matters worse, a scuffle had broken out as a scruffy young man had tried to escape the clutches of three guards and rush towards the crater's edge.

The ugliest-looking cat that the king had ever seen was clinging with sharp claws to one of the guards' legs, and the crowd was screaming at the guards, "Let him go, you bullies!"

To complete the bizarre scene, a strange-looking bat-like creature kept diving into and re-emerging from the crater, wailing a high-pitched scream each time it appeared at the surface.

The king was losing control and the situation was about to get ugly. He shouted to the guards to let the boy go.

Immediately, Pod rushed to the crater's edge, dropped to his knees and began shouting Molly's name. The ugly cat soon joined the boy and began to screech a noise so horrible that the king and most of the crowd had to clutch their ears in pain.

The shouting and screeching had two effects. First, they shocked the crowd into silence and eased the tension slightly as the onlookers felt the grief of the three strange friends gathered at the crater's edge. Second, and far more importantly, the sound of her friends' hurt and grief began to penetrate the fog of Molly's mind. She was lost and had given up, and the timing of her demise only depended on how much strength remained in her arms. For the time being, they were refusing to give up and she still clung resolutely to the Rord.

Slowly, her friends' desperate cries began to stir something in Molly's soul. An inner strength seeped through her tiny battered frame and a determination began to develop deep within. Suddenly, another voice joined the call. Molly, in her semi-awareness, was sure that it was Carnaverous. His voice sounded almost musical. It encouraged Molly and offered her strength. Slowly, a warmth spread through her body, making her feel at least a little stronger.

Molly snapped her eyes open. She could hear clearly her friends' voices from the surface now. Their pain and anguish were enough to push Molly on. She couldn't bear to hear her friends so upset and couldn't bear to be the cause of their grief. Gradually, she began to shift her weight slightly, backwards and forwards. Imperceptibly at first, the Rord began to move. Inch by inch, it started to swing, each sweep a little wider than the one before and the side of the crater a little closer on each swing.

A bigger swing by Molly took the Rord closer to the crater wall and she made a grasp for the rock face. She managed to catch hold of some rocks with her fingertips, but they came away in her hand and she was swinging again. Finally, after a big effort, she slammed into the wall, grabbed hold of the biggest rock with all her might and clung on for dear life. The rock held firm. She had survived. Relief flooded through her and she took her time, inhaled deeply, and took a few minutes to compose herself and consider what to do next. She faced a big climb to the surface and it was not going to be easy.

Pod was shouting himself hoarse as hot tears flowed freely down his face. He refused to believe that Molly was gone. It can't be true, he thought. How am I going to survive without her? He was inconsolable, his grief matched by that of Mank and Ratabat, who lay exhausted in the moon dust, the continued rescue attempts having exhausted the baby bat.

The king had seen enough. He felt no remorse and was embarrassed by the sights before him. He called for Chunky and told the Moon Monkey to get rid of the pathetic show in front of him and do it quickly. Chunky could not have been more pleased. Not only had he finally got rid of Molly, he could now take care of her annoying pesky friends, once and for all. Leaping high and across the arena perimeter, he landed close behind Pod. He charged towards Pod who, lost in his own anguish, was completely unaware of what was about to happen.

Out of the blue, a mouldy piece of moon fruit struck Chunky square on the side of his head, thrown by someone in the crowd who was clearly unhappy with this attempted unprovoked attack. The accurate shot worked perfectly in Pod's favour, as Chunky's huge foot missed him by inches. Had it connected as Chunky desired, then Pod would have been joining Molly.

Instead, Pod was galvanised into action. He leapt to his feet and stood in a defensive position, ready to fight for his life. But the crowd was having none of it. Following the lead of the first fruit thrower, the crowd began to hurl anything and everything at Chunky.

"Leave the boy alone," someone shouted, and this cry was soon taken up by many of the remaining spectators, as a variety of unsavoury items rained down on the Moon Monkey.

Enraged, Chunky bared his teeth and snarled. He rushed towards the crowd, ready to tear each and every one of them to pieces. Suddenly, two of the king's finest guards grabbed Chunky by the arms and began dragging him, screaming and shouting, back towards the king's palace.

The king was furious; Chunky would need to learn restraint and control. King Rufus knew just how to bring Chunky back in line and the unfortunate Moon Monkey was in for an uncomfortable hour or two. A little torture later on would relieve the king's stress and teach Chunky a lesson, just to remind him who was boss.

CHAPTER THIRTY-FOUR

Meanwhile, Molly was also in an uncomfortable position, clinging to the rock precipice for dear life. Not able to see her hands in the pitch blackness, she was petrified that one wrong move could send her tumbling into the abyss. However, she couldn't stay where she was forever. She was dangerously weak and it wouldn't be long before she drifted back into unconsciousness. She knew she had to move but had no idea where to.

Mustering her last reserves of strength, she reached out and grabbed a rock. Gently applying her weight, she was not surprised when the rock broke away and hurtled down into the depths. Frustrated, she screamed. In this darkness, she would never escape and there would be no rescue party as everyone on the surface assumed she was already dead.

Thinking of her friends spurred Molly on. She reached out again, found a firm handhold and gradually pulled herself forward. This time the rock held strong and she inched upwards. But she was weak and at this slow pace she would never survive and she couldn't see her next move.

Despondent, she was about to give up when she heard a low hum, quiet at first but slowly getting louder. Something was coming towards her, but she had no idea what.

It was just then that something amazing occurred: a faint fluorescent light appeared on the rock face. Illuminating a perfect hole, ideal for Molly's next move, she had no hesitation in using it. Once she was safely positioned, the strange light moved up the rock face and lit up another perfect foothold. Molly was now on the move but what or who her unlikely saviour was, she did not know.

Determined to find out, she called out into the darkness. "Thank you so much," she cried. "But, please, show yourself. I would like to see my hero!"

The light dimmed and went out. For a second, Molly thought she had scared her rescuer off, but she needn't have worried. Suddenly, the crater was illuminated inches from her face. Molly recoiled in fright; it was a mythical creature called a Rant. The creature had a fierce head with long antennae, huge eyes and large pincer-like jaws. The Rant's abdomen could emit a low hum and, when required, produce a bright fluorescent light. It was this light that was now helping Molly to find her way.

The Rant was a very ancient creature rumoured to have walked the moon craters since the beginning of time. It had been held in great esteem by the ancient moon miners, who used the Rant's powers to find their way around the mines. This particular Rant was very interested in the Rord and, after approaching Molly with caution, it rubbed itself along the Rord, rather like Mank, when he had an irritating itch.

Contact with the Rord appeared to have a strange effect on the creature; the dull hum changed to magical notes that lifted and fell in perfect harmony. Its abdomen shimmered and sparkled and grew brighter and brighter.

Suddenly, out of the darkness, another light appeared on the other side of the crater. It was another Rant. This one began to flash. Molly's rescuer followed suit, and each flashed to the other. To Molly, it appeared as though they were sending each other messages. Out of the depths of the crater another light appeared, swiftly followed by another. With each new light, the magical tune grew louder as each Rant added its own notes to the chorus. Soon there were dozens of lights and a beautiful orchestra of sound.

Slowly, the lights approached Molly and it wasn't long before she could make out the shapes and bodies of the Rants. She no longer felt scared, as she could feel that the creatures meant her no harm. One by one, they approached her and the Rord, each taking the opportunity to rub itself on the mystical rope. This strange attention was also having an impact on the Rord and Molly could feel the power surging through her precious gift. The Rants were ecstatic in its presence and their joy was overwhelming.

The effect was dramatic. The crater was lit brighter than the surface of the Moon and Molly could see every nook and cranny; even the darkest crevices were illuminated. Offering her thanks and stroking the original Rant, she took another step on the path to safety. She clutched a newly illuminated handhold and pulled herself up a little closer to the surface. As soon as the light further up the crater grew dim, another

Rant scurried past Molly and illuminated her path ahead. Slowly but surely, she was getting painfully closer to safety. Her pain was still evident but her confidence was growing. She could do this.

"Mank! Look! There's a light," exclaimed Pod. He was still at the crater's edge and could now see the fluorescent light emanating from deep within the crater. Springing into action, he ran to the perimeter fencing, ripped off a section of rope and hurried back. Gradually, he lowered the rope into the crater.

It was a little short but Molly was relieved to see the salvation that Pod offered. The rope was just a little out of reach but, with the light of the Rants, she quickly scurried the last few feet and lunged for the dangling end. She clasped hold of the rope and hung on for dear life; she was now dangling once again over the abyss. With a flick of her wrist, she unravelled the Rord from its previous holding place and rewound the precious coil around her waist. Now she was ready and she just needed the person on the other end of the rope to help her up.

Feeling a weight on the end of the rope, Pod began to pull as hard as he could. Molly felt vulnerable dangling in the air like that and it seemed at first as if nothing was happening. But, bit by bit, she started to rise up towards the crater entrance and the Moon's surface. The Rants scaled the rocks each side of the crater, helping to light the way.

"Help me," cried Pod, struggling to pull the rope up on his own. "It's Molly," he shouted. "She's alive. I know it."

The king, already halfway back to his quarters and some much-needed refreshments, heard Pod's cries. Now what? he thought. What else can go wrong? But his interest was stirred. He scurried back to the arena. When he saw Pod and heard his words, he ordered two guards to help the struggling boy. Could it be? he thought. Could that amazing brave young girl still be alive? If it were true, it would be perfect. With the disappearance of Carnaverous, the king was missing an important cog in his master plan.

Time for Molly seemed to stand still and her progress seemed unbelievably slow. All of a sudden, the speed of her ascent increased dramatically as the guards helped Pod to pull the rope up. Molly could now make out the silhouettes of her rescuers. She could see Pod. She had survived the crater and was seconds from the Moon's surface. She turned to shout her thanks to the Rants who, having seen that Molly was safe, were now scurrying back into the depths. Only her original saviour remained, determined to ensure that Molly reached safety.

She reached out and stroked the Rant's head. The creature seemed to enjoy this, as it nodded its head in appreciation and its abdomen sparkled. The Rant then opened its large jaws and dropped a small pebble into Molly's hand. It was smooth and shiny and was completely covered in an elaborate design. Molly had little time to investigate further and dropped the pebble into her pocket. At that moment, two burly arms wrapped around Molly and hoisted her to the surface. The Rant disappeared and Molly collapsed onto the ground.

Pod rushed to Molly, wrapped his arms around her and hugged her tight.

"Calm down," whispered Molly. "I didn't survive the crater just to get crushed by you."

Releasing his grip a little, Pod began to laugh. Mank charged up then and joined in by licking Molly's face.

Molly's joy and happiness were short-lived, however. As soon as she began to relax into Pod's arms, the guards who had helped in rescuing her now pushed Pod out of the way. He tried to protect Molly, leaping to her defence. The guards were veterans and specially trained in close combat; they simply lifted Pod up and threw him. He clattered into a tree, which he hit hard. He promptly slid to the ground, stunned. The guards grabbed Molly. Although she struggled, she was totally exhausted. The men began to drag her away.

Molly was taken straight to the king, who grabbed her by the chin and stared into her face. For an instant, a spark of recognition passed between the two but it was gone in a second. Shaking his head clear, the king ordered the guards to take Molly to the winner's enclosure.

"What?" blurted Molly. "But I didn't win!"

"Yes," said the king slyly. "But Carnaverous has disappeared and I need a winner. So, my girl, as runner-up, it is you."

"Hurry along now," shouted the king to his guards.

Pod, who was watching the proceedings, couldn't believe his eyes or ears. He rose slowly on unsteady legs and shouted, "Molly's won. She's been declared the winner. Hurrah for Molly!"

The remaining crowd soon began to take up the chant. "Hurrah for Molly!"

Pod slid back to the ground, content in the knowledge that they were going to be rich. The king had promised great riches to the winners and now Molly was among them. Pod was positive that Molly would share the rewards with her friends.

The king had a very different idea of what the rewards might be, but all that would come later. Before that, he had some celebrations to enjoy. The finals were very nearly over and the king had speeches to make and plans to fulfil.

CHAPTER THIRTY-FIVE

The large courtyard was surrounded on all sides by a high solid wall with large turrets on each corner. Elite soldiers stood all along the top of the high walls. They appeared relaxed but were on high alert. The tournament winners were all crammed inside. They chattered excitedly to each other, expecting to be greatly honoured. Chunky looked huge and menacing, while the strange hooded archer from the dark side casually cleaned his bow and looked a little bored. In addition to the winners, the king had his scouts invite the most gifted and talented of the losers, including Sally Lion Head.

A hush fell over the crowd as the king appeared atop of the high wall, flanked by his two most trusted generals. All three looked resplendent in their finery. The king now wore a large feathered hat made from the rarest moomu bird feathers. Purple and red in colour, the top of the feathers had what looked like elaborate eyes painted on them. Molly thought they were the most beautiful feathers she had ever seen. They made the king look instantly taller and more menacing. He was hard to miss, exactly the effect that Rufus was after.

"Welcome all. Congratulations, my winners," he boomed. "You have all fought and battled without equal. You are my champions, the finest fighters on the planet Moon and my loyal and trusted servants. Your reward will be beyond compare. Each and every one of you deserves your place in my humble courtyard. Tomorrow, I will hand out your medals and awards. But tonight, we party!"

Before today, Molly had only heard rumours of the mythical Rants. Now, she was about to meet these strange creatures twice in only a few hours. Five of the poor creatures were led on chains onto the stage below the king. Behind them were their carers who were skilled musicians or, in Molly's mind, slave-masters.

Once in position, the carers produced two short sticks from a holder sheathed to their legs. They began to hit the Rants on their abdomens with the short sticks. Instantly, the Rants began to glow and a mystical magical tune emitted from their bodies. The crowd was entranced. The music was stunning, uplifting and crystal-clear.

The assembled crowd began to sway and then dance, almost trance-like. Molly couldn't help but be impressed, but she was not happy with the treatment meted out to the captured Rants and vowed to help them if she could. She wanted to return the favour to the crater Rants who had helped to save her. But for now, that would have to wait, as the king was clearly intent on everyone enjoying the occasion.

Waiters and servants appeared in a long procession and began to wind through the crowd. Each one held a silver platter aloft, which glimmered and shimmered in the moonlight. Each platter carried numerous delightful nibbles and canapés. Molly had no idea what they were but each one tasted better than the last. Most of the trays also contained drinks of every shape and size. Molly was well aware of the effects of moonshine, so she only sipped at her exquisite drink. It was like liquid nectar and very addictive, so she would need to keep her wits about her. The same could not be said of her fellow contestants who were clearly enjoying the king's hospitality a little too much. Molly couldn't help but worry that this was what the king intended and that something sinister was afoot.

From that moment, she refused to consume any more food or drink. This was a very wise decision as, unbeknown to her, the king had added a little something extra to the food and drink, just to make sure that the party went with a bang.

It was the early hours of the morning when Molly first noticed a subtle change in the courtyard. Most of her fellow victors were sprawled out on the floor exactly where they had fallen. A few, with obviously stronger constitutions, were still attempting to dance, although swaying would have been a more appropriate description of what they were doing. Some were occupying themselves in other ways and Molly swiftly averted her eyes. As she looked away, she noticed that a guard was busy hammering nails into a big beam of wood on one of the exit doors, firmly securing it shut.

Alarmed, Molly made her way to the next exit and was horrified to find that that door was also being hammered closed. What was happening? She rushed across the courtyard. Now she was very concerned. The doors on that side had already been well and truly fixed shut. With the front sealed and now both sides in the process of being closed shut, Molly needed help. She was desperate.

She rushed to the nearest group of revellers and tried to rouse them. She grabbed the one closest to her and shook him as hard as she could but to no avail; he was totally out of it. The king's extra ingredient was clearly having the desired effect. She moved to the next couple and her interruptions were not appreciated. She was roughly pushed away before the couple recommenced their romancing.

Molly tried to scream and shout but was only met with cries of "Pipe down" and "Shut the noise".

It was hopeless. She would get no help from her fellow contestants. The drugged food, drink and hypnotic dancing had all worked a charm. She was in this alone and needed to escape. With her mind made up, and determined not to draw attention to herself, she crept as quickly as she could to the rear of the courtyard. She was in luck. At the back there was a single door, open and unguarded.

CHAPTER THIRTY-SIX

Molly knew she had to get help. She didn't know what was happening but she knew that all the competition winners and the best of the losers were now imprisoned. She inched her way to the door. The path was clear but, just as she was about to make a run for it, a guard appeared. Molly dropped to the ground, cuddled up to the nearest drunken reveller and played unconscious. The man didn't smell too good and Molly had to hold her breath. Luckily, the guard had other things on his mind and marched quickly past. Molly took her chance, leapt to her feet and made a dash for the door, passing through without hindrance. She was nearly free.

Nearly, however, is never enough and just as she thought she had escaped, a huge arm scooped her into the air and into the ugly face of Chunky the Moon Monkey. Her head jolted back. The drunken reveller's breath may have been bad, but it was nothing compared to Chunky's. Molly nearly passed out.

One of Chunky's punishments for not dealing with

Pod correctly was having to complete guard duty. The king had refused Chunky permission to join the party and instead made him sentry for the entire night. Needless to say, Chunky was not in the best of moods. The air in Molly's lungs whooshed out as Chunky squeezed tight.

"Where do you think you are going, little one?" hissed Chunky. "The king has plans and, unfortunately, even you are needed. My plans for you will have to wait."

Molly had no time to absorb these words as Chunky launched her back into the courtyard with one of his big Moon Monkey feet. She flew with the greatest of ease and her fall was broken by a group of drunken revellers lying sprawled on the floor. Untangling herself, she struggled back to her feet. But it was too late. Where freedom beckoned only seconds before, now she was trapped as the final gate was hammered shut.

Along with everyone else in the courtyard, Molly was now a prisoner of the king. She could do nothing but sit and wait for morning. Who knew what the king had in mind for them all?

CHAPTER THIRTY-SEVEN

For Molly, time seemed to stop and it was not an early morning start. Most of the revellers slept late and were very slow to realise their predicament. Gradually, as the morning progressed and the revellers came to their senses, awareness began to kick in. At first, a couple of the contestants tried to leave only to discover that all the exits were locked tight. Soon a sense of anger spread across the crowd as people woke up to find others shaking them and passing on the news that they were imprisoned.

Clearing the fog in their minds, and with Molly helping to organise, a party of about fifteen began to co-ordinate an escape attempt. They stormed the main exit but the guards were well armed and, although skirmishes broke out, the guards collectively pushed the attempted escapees back. Molly found a spear held across her chest as two guards used their considerable weight to push her back towards the centre of the courtyard. Anger began to turn to fear and panic. Where were their trophies and promised riches, now their hard work was being rewarded with treachery? Shouts and cries spread across the courtyard.

At first, there were random cries, including "Where's our rewards?" and "Let us go!" but gradually the individual shouts developed into one loud chorus of "We want the king. We want the king!"

Buried deep within the castle, the king was enjoying a late breakfast and was not happy to be disturbed. "What?" he spluttered through a mouthful of moon hog. "I'm busy!"

It was left to an unfortunate servant to break the news that the newly assembled captives were more than a little unhappy.

"Let them sweat," said the king. "I am finishing my breakfast and I will see them when I am ready, not when they demand!" With this, he gave the poor lad a quick slap around the ear for good measure. "Now get out!"

Back in the courtyard things were starting to turn ugly. The wrestling champion, a short stout mwarf, had no desire to remain captive. His escape was going well and he had felled two guards, killing one stone dead while the other lay mortally wounded. The mwarf was strong and determined and was making headway when three of the archers on the ramparts let loose their arrows. All three arrows struck deep in the mwarf's back, bringing the poor creature to his knees. Chunky picked up the dead guard's axe and swiftly sent the mwarf's head spinning through the air, as the rest of his body fell into the dirt. The remaining captives were stunned, horrified that the mwarf had been killed.

"Now, all of you, quiet!" bellowed Chunky. "You will wait to hear the king's words."

Out of the silence came the sound of a single handclap. It was the king. "Hear, hear, Chunky, very well said."

As one, the captives turned to face the king. Their anger and frustration radiated out, but the king was oblivious to the cries, shouts and insults that they directed at him. He merely raised his arms for quiet and patiently waited for the outburst to calm down.

When Rufus was ready, and not a moment sooner, he began to reveal his true plans and launched into a well-rehearsed speech. "Citizens and loyal subjects, you are my champions and worthy winners. Each and every one of you has excelled at the tournament. You are the finest athletes and warriors that the Moon has to offer.

"Your King and Country have grave need of your unique services. The rewards that I have promised will be yours, every single one of you. I am a man of my word but first I ask a task of you all, just one more small favour and your lives will change forever. You will be rich beyond compare and your names will go down in history.

"Your Moon needs you and we need revenge, for we have all been violated. Many years ago, in the reign of my father, we were invaded. It is now time to avenge this sacrilege. It is our turn.

"Revenge will be mine! For too long we have sat in the shadow of their pretty colours. We are going to conquer the patterned planet!"

Collectively, every jaw in the courtyard dropped.

Disbelief, shock and horror spread like wildfire among the assembled captives. One individual, Molly didn't know who, was brave enough to shout out, "You're mad!"

Retribution was swift. Two guards rushed into the crowd. One punched the perpetrator hard in the stomach and he was swiftly brought to his knees.

"Now, now," the king continued. "While this is a shock to you all, it is going to happen. I demand it. Victory will be mine! The rewards will be yours. However, if you oppose me then I am afraid a lifetime of torture and misery awaits, courtesy of my finest dungeons. You all have the choice, but I strongly recommend my first option."

Molly went weak at the knees. This was madness. The king had gone too far and really had lost the plot. Many of the strange things that had been happening lately now began to make sense – the hushed conversations that she had overheard, the searches of the districts, increased army activity, rumours circulating in the moozers. The king had to be stopped. Molly didn't know why, but her every instinct told her that the king's plans would lead to disaster for the Moon's inhabitants. Unfortunately, Molly had no idea how to stop him!

The king was still rambling on. Having consulted his scientists, the most favourable time for the invasion to take place was in three days from now. The patterned planet, the Glorb, that large burning orb that gave the Moon light and heat, and the Moon would all be in alignment. This was a rare planetary occurrence when the Moon would be at its closest to the patterned planet, offering the best chance of success. The crowd stood shocked and silent – three days was so soon. This was complete madness. Many thought that the plan was doomed to fail and that the king would never succeed. Despite this, the alternative, a life in the dungeons, was infinitely worse. So, when the king asked for those who disagreed with or opposed him to step forward, no one did. They all thought that they would take their chances and, if they somehow survived, the rewards would be well worth the pain.

The king, seeing that no one openly disagreed with his plans, sat down with a smug smile on his face. Perfect, he thought. My plans are well and truly unleashed! I will be remembered forever!

CHAPTER THIRTY-EIGHT

The king's most senior general then stood up and rather sadly declared that the days ahead would involve training and preparation for the upcoming invasion. The guards then moved among the crowd and divided people into smaller, more manageable groups. Molly and Sally Lion Head were allocated to the same team. Although Molly had defeated and injured Sally, the Lion Head seemed to bear no grudge. Her injuries were healing and her tail, although not quite as long and fluffy as before, had begun to show signs of growing back. Molly felt it was good to have an acquaintance, if not quite a friend, in her team. Molly had little choice in the matter and could only go along with the training. Any suspected lack of effort was immediately corrected with a swift whack on the back of the legs. The only good thing was the food and drink. The king was determined that his new attack force would be in the best possible condition and everyone knew that an army cannot march on an empty stomach. Fine food and refreshments were available all the time and Molly took the opportunity to stock up while she still could.

The training was punishing and at the end of the day Molly all but collapsed, exhausted, onto a pile of straw which served as her makeshift bedding. Despite her worries for the future, she fell soundly asleep.

Later in the night, she became aware of something nibbling at her ear. Still asleep, she tried to swat the annoyance away but the irritation continued. Slowly opening one eye and then the other, Molly was amazed to discover that it was Ratabat, who had flown over the high walls, past the guards and found her. Warmth and emotion flowed through her body. She was so pleased that her little friend had found her.

Poor Ratabat nearly suffocated under all of Molly's well-meaning attention. Molly couldn't contain her feelings any longer and tears began to flow. Ratabat flapped and hopped around and although it couldn't talk, it tried its best to communicate understanding and love.

Molly stroked the bat's tiny head and whispered her thoughts and concerns into its ear. Forcing herself to think, she tried to plan a way to get a message to Pod and the outside. Unfortunately, she had no way of communicating and Ratabat would be unable to carry anything too heavy. In the end, all she could think of was to pluck a few strands of her hair and to ask Ratabat to take it to Pod. That way, at least, he would know that she was alive. After several attempts, she was hopeful that Ratabat finally understood her plan. Reluctantly and tearfully, Molly said farewell to Ratabat and forced her little friend to fly away.

It took Molly a long time to fall back to sleep. She was

worried and fitful, and she tossed and turned. Eventually, however, she drifted away. Suddenly, Carnaverous appeared in her dream. Lifelike and loud, it seemed to Molly as if he was really standing there next to her.

"The king must be stopped, Molly," whispered the great man. "His actions, if they succeed, will have very grave consequences for the Moon. This I have foreseen."

"How can I stop him?" she asked. "I am but a frightened little girl."

"No!" roared Carnaverous, getting angry in a flash. "You are amazing, courageous and strong, and I need your help." Cryptically, he continued, "You are the Moon's future. Your people need you."

"How?" she asked. "How can I possibly stop him and his entire army?"

"I don't know yet," sighed Carnaverous. "But be ready. You are not alone. Others are with you."

With these words ringing in her head, Carnaverous disappeared as quickly as he had appeared. Molly woke up and was unable to return to sleep. She spent the rest of the night pondering his words and their meaning.

The next morning, it was a very tired Molly who showed up for training, a fact quickly noticed by her trainers and which led to a nasty beating at their hands.

CHAPTER THIRTY-NINE

Ratabat, who had flown magnificently, had managed to track down Pod. Unfortunately, Pod was also being held prisoner. Mad Angel had spotted Pod at the crater edge, trying to save Molly. While the guards were busy, she had grabbed the lad by the ear and practically dragged him back to their home. Pod was soon put to work and was, at that very moment, literally chained to the kitchen sink. Angel mustn't have cleaned up for weeks and Pod faced a veritable mountain of pots and pans, all of them filthy. Ratabat flew to Pod and landed on the tap in front of him, shaking its head from side to side.

Pod could see something in the bat's mouth. "What is it?" he asked, and Ratabat opened its small mouth and dropped the strands of hair into the water in the sink. Puzzled at first, Pod didn't understand. Gradually, however, recognition dawned. He recognised that colour. He knew whose hair it was. Molly was alive.

"Thank the stars," said Pod. "But where is she?"

Ratabat could only respond by jumping up and down on the tap.

"I know," said Pod. "I think she is in trouble."

Ratty jumped quicker at this. Unfortunately, in his current predicament, Pod was not in a position to help Molly at all.

"Find Mank," Pod said to Ratabat. "Go back to the Sate. Stay hidden and safe. As soon as I can, I will escape, come and find you and rescue Molly."

Saying those words made Pod feel brave and sure but deep down he knew that turning this statement into reality would be very difficult. Thankfully, Ratabat seemed to understand. He circled a couple of times and flew off.

CHAPTER FORTY

The trapped competitors were watched closely at all times. Molly had no escape and no choice; she had to go along with the king's wishes. She was constantly kept busy and, much to her dismay, time flew by. The day of the proposed attack was almost upon them. The assembled captives were put through their paces again in the morning but in the afternoon, things changed.

Training ceased and they were all led into the great hall, which was now filled with seats with a stage at the far end. Upon the stage, in front of charts, formulas and plans, sat the king's generals, the most influential and prominent people of the realm. Next to them sat the finest knights. Next to them were the best scientists. Next to them the mystics. And next to them the tacticians. Sitting in front of them all was the king.

King Rufus stood and addressed the crowd. "My heroes, my warriors. Time is nearly upon us. Greatness is within your grasp. It is now time to reveal my plans in detail. Each and every one of you has an important role to play and now you will discover what that role is."

Before the king had finished speaking, Molly was grabbed by the arm and roughly pushed through a door leading to an adjacent room. Others were also being led or pushed into the same space. At first, it was a little cramped and Molly struggled to see who else was there, but slowly people spread across the room. Molly counted thirty or so people. A hand suddenly grabbed Molly and dragged her to a corner. It was Sally Lion Head. Molly was relieved; she had at least one ally in the room. But her joy was short-lived and followed by her worst nightmare. A huge presence appeared in the doorway, practically blocking the entrance. It was Chunky. The enormous Moon Monkey moved to the front of the room, puffing out his chest.

Chunky knew that the eyes of the room were on him. Clearing his throat to speak, he let everyone know that he was in charge. He paused for effect, while the room fell silent.

"You, my friends, are the luckiest of the lucky," he declared. He had obviously been coached on what to say, for he wasn't the brightest tool in the box. "We are the most important group in the king's grand plan, for we are the initial invasion landing party! Yes, my friends, we will be the first people from the Moon to ever land on the patterned planet. I will now hand you over to the king's chief tactical general."

Chunky then sat down, extremely pleased with himself. He had spent the last few days trying to remember these words and this was the first time that he had got them all right and in the correct order.

The door opened and in walked General Clutterberry, the king's chief advisor and the person that Molly had seen with the king in the enchanted garden all those weeks ago. He was a large man, whose once-toned body was beginning to sag. His face was dominated by a large handlebar moustache and a thick greying beard. Although it would take a brave person to tell him that it was grey. He was instantly recognisable.

General Clutterberry was not a man to be messed with and the assembled group was slightly in awe. His reputation was fearsome and he did not suffer fools. As a result, all eyes were on him. No one was brave enough to say anything; every person in the room had heard the tales. Only torture and pain faced those that opposed the general and he was very very strict. He lifted his arm and began to outline the details of the king's daring plan. It was madness, but Molly could not deny that the scheme was brilliant. The Moon's finest brains had worked for years to put this invasion in place and the plan was detailed and thorough.

Molly and the others in the room had been selected as the advance landing party. Molly's jaw dropped at the idea that they were going to be the first people from the Moon to ever land on the patterned pattern. They were going to be adventurers, pioneers and, in different circumstances, Molly would have been overwhelmed with excitement. Unfortunately, the reasons behind the audacious landing attempt were all wrong. Molly knew more than ever that she had to stop them, for, until now, she had thought the invasion impossible and that it would never work.

After the initial shock, and once the shouts, murmurs and general mayhem had calmed down, General Clutterberry began to outline more detailed plans. The moon scientists had built an interstellar transporter, a large cylindrical device that could, if it worked correctly, propel the people in this room thousands of miles across space and time to a different world.

Molly prayed that the calculations were correct. If not, the outcome would be disastrous for the thirty people it would propel to the new world. Molly gulped. Once they had successfully landed on the patterned planet, the invasion party would secure the landing zone perimeter. With the perimeter secure, Molly, with help from Chunky and Sally Lion Head, would build an amplifier which would boost the power of the interstellar transporter. If the booster worked, then the rest of the king's army could travel across space to land on the patterned planet and the invasion would take place. The king was assured of success but Molly could see only death, carnage and catastrophe.

A deep feeling of dread gnawed at her insides but she had no time to ponder the plans. Chunky roughly grabbed her arm as she and Sally Lion Head were shoved to the front of the room.

General Clutterberry looked down at them and shook his head. "The whole mission depends on you three. I think the king is mad, but he reckons that you three are the best that the Moon can offer." Still shaking his head, wearily, the general rolled out a map on the table in front of the three. "This," said the general, "is the landing zone! Over many years, the king's advisors and scientists have looked through archives and old documents, some centuries old. They were looking for clues, something that would help them to discover how the patterned people landed on our Moon. The king's belief is that if they could come and invade us, there must be a way of reversing the process so we could invade them. After many decades of searching, they succeeded. This map is just a part of the discovery and has been reproduced from documents that are thousands of years old."

The general paused for breath and then continued. "It has been discovered that, centuries ago, an ancient civilisation built a large circle of stones in a land called Briton. A land of savages, conflict and unrest, and the purpose and origins of the stones are shrouded in mystery. Over time, the ancient civilisation gradually died out, and the reason for the circle, how it was built and its uses were lost to history. The strange patterned people began to believe that the stone circle was dedicated to the Glorb and its worship. The king's scientists discovered that this was incorrect and couldn't be further from the truth. The ancient stones were, in fact, dedicated to the Moon. The ancient circle's name was Stonehenge."

This information had amused the king greatly. He frequently referred to the inhabitants of the patterned planet as stupid. They had no idea of the true meaning of these stones or the power they possessed. This was one of the reasons why he was convinced he would win.

It had taken many years and much research, but the king had discovered the truth about the stones and their potential. Each individual stone was very powerful and this power was further enhanced if the stones were connected together. The moon scientists had managed to harness the energy of two of the stones but could not connect to the others. This, they had calculated, was enough power to allow the small landing party to travel across space, and it would be Molly's and Sally's role to connect all of the stones together. Using their skills as crater walkers, both would help each other to walk tightrope-style across the gaps between the stones, linking them up.

For someone as skilled as Molly, this would be relatively easy, but not even the scientists could predict the differing conditions that the patterned pattern offered. Both Molly and Sally would be carrying delicate equipment and it would be dark, which would make the task much more difficult and maybe the simple would prove impossible.

Once Molly and Sally had completed the task to connect the giant monoliths, the combined power would be immense. This power would open a larger portal to the Moon and possibly other worlds as well. This larger portal would allow the king's army to invade and conquer.

Molly felt dizzy. Her knees were weak and she reached out to grab hold of Sally Lion Head. War was coming and the relative peace of the Moon was about to be shattered, possibly forever. She was not as confident as the king in the invasion's success. If it failed, it would be all her fault. If she achieved her tasks, she would be responsible for the invasion of another world. It was too much to bear. The burden was too great and Molly's shoulders sagged. She could not let this happen. Molly did not want to go down in history as the little girl who brought death and misery to two worlds.

Sally helped to prop Molly up. Luckily, the general had not noticed and was now moving on to other parts of the plan. To Molly it was all a blur. She was lost in despair and pain.

"Get a grip," whispered Sally Lion Head. "We need you. You must believe that you can stop this madness. You have the power to change history but that could be for the good and not just the bad. C'mon, Molly." She squeezed Molly's arm. "Be positive. The invasion rests on us and if we can prevent the army landing on the patterned planet then the king's plans will fail before they have even begun."

Sally's words offered Molly a few crumbs of comfort. Lion Head was right. But what could the pair of them achieve on their own?

It was then that the familiar voice of Carnaverous once again entered Molly's mind. "You are never alone," whispered the voice. "I will be by your side and I will help you. I have the beginnings of a plan," Carnaverous continued. "I had to wait to see how the king proposed to start his invasion. Now that I know, I can start working to stop him. Fear not, Molly. When the time comes, I will talk to you."

"Wake up," screamed Chunky right in Molly's face. "Pay attention."

Molly was swiftly brought back to the present as Chunky shook her.

"This is no time for daydreaming."

Feeling a little relieved and with the words of

Carnaverous echoing in her mind, Molly forcefully pushed Chunky away. "Leave me alone, you bully," she cried.

Chunky, not used to such insolence from such a pathetic creature, raised his huge arms, ready to batter Molly.

"Stop that!" barked the general. "This is important. We do not have time for arguments among ourselves. Get back here, Chunky. Now! And that's an order!"

Reluctantly, Chunky moved back to the general's side, but not before he whispered to Molly, "You're mine. I'll get you for this, once and for all."

General Clutterberry had all but finished outlining his plans and was engaged in one last patriotic rant about history in the making and that we would make the Moon proud. With one final theatrical wave of his arms, his huge moustache wiggled and waggled, and the general left the room as quickly as he'd entered. No one made a sound. The entire room was in shock and disbelief.

It was time for Chunky and the guards to usher the leading invasion party back into the great hall to join the rest of the assembled task force. Molly soon gathered that each section of the new army had been led to separate rooms and told of their roles. On their return to the great hall, they found tables laden with food and drink. There was no alcohol, however, as the king wanted everyone alert and ready early the next morning. Although the food was plentiful and splendid, the king only allowed one plateful per person. He wanted everyone on the top of their game and no one suffering from overindulgence.

Talk in the hall was of only one thing – the invasion.

Molly was horrified to discover that many of her fellow competitors were happy and honoured to have these new positions of importance and value. But there were just as many who were horrified. These people found themselves drawn to Molly and Sally Lion Head. They began to think that Molly could save them. Molly and Sally Lion Head would be among the first of the opposers to land on the patterned planet. In order to stop the invasion, the early task force would need to be involved.

Molly did not like the responsibility that now rested on her tiny shoulders but even she couldn't deny that the future of her people lay in her hands. The weight of the world lay heavily on her conscience.

Chunky had no such concerns and his only thought was his stomach. He hadn't taken the one plate of food rule well. At that moment, he was causing a scene, continually trying to steal food from other people's plates. A couple of the mwarves were not happy, and steadfastly refused to give up their roasted moonhog liver to the greedy Moon Monkey. A scuffle broke out and rapidly spread. Even the Samhain Mages, who generally kept to themselves, got involved. Chunky had tried to steal a loaf of bread from one of them, but a ball of fire had shot out from the sleeve of the Samhain Mage's cloak.

Without warning, Chunky's massive Moon Monkey bum was on fire. He waved his long arms about manically and screeched in pain as he spun around the room trying to put the fire out. Anyone in the way was knocked flying by the spinning, burning Monkey mountain. Two guards rushed in, each carrying a bucket of water that they promptly threw over the shocked Chunky. He slumped to the ground, absolutely drenched. Other guards quickly restored calm over anyone still squabbling over the food.

The king and General Clutterberry reappeared and declared lights out. It was to be an early night for everyone. The king wanted everyone to be bright and alert for the early start in the morning. The general then declared that the first landing party would enter the transporter at 2.53am. It had been calculated by the brains that this would ensure that they landed at Stonehenge at 4.15am, patterned planet time. This would be an hour before patterned planet dawn. Under the cover of darkness, the landing party would set the boosters to allow the main invading force through. The full invasion would begin at dawn.

CHAPTER FORTY-ONE

The troops were led to their confined quarters and to bed. Molly was in no mood to sleep and spent hours tossing and turning. Judging by the whispers and chatter, many others also struggled to calm down and sleep. Gradually, however, the rooms stilled and quiet spread through the halls. Eventually, Molly too dropped off. This was the calm before the storm.

Molly suddenly sat bolt upright. Her short sleep was well and truly over. The guards were ringing loud bells directly into the ears of those who, despite the din, were still asleep. The guards went around by candlelight ensuring that everyone was up and getting battle-ready. It was nearly time. Invasion day was upon them. With hardly a minute to collect her thoughts, Molly and the lead task force were led to the armoury.

General Clutterberry stood waiting, his big arms crossed and his moustache twitching in the eerie dim light. "Now, my heroes," he mirthlessly chuckled, "because of the importance of your mission and the fact that some of you are not too enthusiastic…of course, we trust you, but…" and the moustache seemed to laugh at this, "you will each be assigned a guard to keep a watchful eye on you. The least trustworthy will be looked after by the toughest guards," he continued. "We need to do everything to ensure the success of the mission."

With this, Molly's dreaded day suddenly got a whole lot worse. Out of nowhere, Chunky slapped Molly on the shoulder.

"Aren't you the lucky one," he growled. "I'm your guard. Oh, and after you have completed the task, I have grand plans for you." Grimly, Chunky then whispered, "Enjoy your last day on the Moon. You will never see it again."

With these grim words echoing in her head, Molly was led to the armoury and given the weapons she would require for the assault. She was given a javarod and a crater rope. The latter was a cheap rough imitation, not nearly as fine as the Rord. Luckily, Molly had the Rord concealed around her middle and the Nitsplitter was safely tucked away in her boot. Each time she had been searched she had managed to distract the guards. Chunky, however, was a much tougher proposition.

As soon as Molly was handed the javarod, Chunky snatched it from her hands and promptly jabbed her in the bum. "I think I will look after this for the time being," he snarled.

Once the task force had been assigned guards and the required weapons, they were led from the armoury down several steps. As they travelled further under the castle, the steps became uneven, damp and slippery. The air was moist, stale and musty. Trickles of water ran down the thick castle walls and Molly became aware of a green fluorescent glow that seemed to originate from the actual walls; it was the algae that grew in these damp cool conditions.

One step was particularly uneven, wet and dangerous. Molly suddenly slipped and found herself dangling over the precipice. She seemed to hover in thin air. Disaster was seconds away when, out of the blue, a huge hairy hand grabbed her shoulder and pulled her back to the step and safety.

"Oh no you don't, little one," snarled Chunky. "You don't get off that lightly. Your destiny is in my hands."

Molly sucked in the damp air and leaned against the dank wall, visibly shaking. She was aware that Chunky had possibly saved her life. It was not a thought that she was comfortable with.

With greater care, the assembled task force continued their descent. Molly gradually became aware of a gentle hum which got louder with each step. It was the castle's generators. Normally, they powered the king's huge residence but, given the use of candles and torches, it was obvious to Molly that the power was being diverted elsewhere.

The noise grew louder the closer they got. The generators' sound was strained and laboured, as if they were operating beyond their capacity.

The party had reached the lowest level and were now being led past the huge shaking generators. Huge columns of smoke wafted up enormous chimneys situated above the machines. Blackened muscular mwarves fed the roaring fires with massive moontree trunks which crackled and spat. The temperature was intense. Molly could feel the heat blistering her skin as she walked past.

The guards, also feeling the heat, hurried the team through a large heavy door and into a great cavern. Ominously, the heavy door closed with a hefty bang behind them and the guards pushed the team further into the room. Molly's jaw dropped and she stood fixed to the spot. In the centre of the room was the strangest contraption she had ever seen. Over many years, the king's scientists had secretly collected the many objects that had landed on the surface of the Moon. Most had originated from the patterned planet, but not all. The king was keen that the general population knew as little as possible about these invasions. As he saw it, they were even more reason for the planned attack. Indeed, Sate, Molly's home, was in fact one of these foreign objects, the remnants of a satellite.

Over the years, these items had been analysed, investigated and logged. Gradually, the scientists began to put the parts together to form the contraption that Molly now stared at.

A large circular metal ring led to a cylindrical tube that disappeared into the darkness of the cavern. The ring was several feet thick. It started at the floor and stretched high up into the roof. It was wide enough to allow four soldiers to stand shoulder to shoulder inside it. Currently, the interior of the ring was intensely black. The ring dominated the room. All along the side of the room stood banks of computers, instruments, dials and knobs. Wires and cables ran all around them, most leading from the ring to the cylindrical tube and from the tube and ring into the banks of computers and instruments. A huge pipe, humming and glowing hot, ran from the generator room into this cavern. Only a leaden gate prevented the energy from coursing into the machine and powering the contraption up. The gate, however, was only just holding the energy back, as the pipe shook and rattled, and screws and rivets buckled loose. Something needed to happen fast or all hell would break loose.

Scientists in white coats scurried around, pushing buttons, adjusting bits and bobs, all the time filling in details on charts. General Clutterberry and several senior scientists stood there looking at graphs and comparing notes. The general's moustache wiggled. Molly was overcome with anxiety. Instantly, a fanfare struck up; from where, Molly had no idea. The space was suddenly illuminated by bright lights, temporarily blinding those gathered. As eyes adjusted and people began to focus, they saw something even more confusing. Many rubbed their eyes in disbelief. The king appeared to be hovering in front of them, above the cylindrical tube. It looked like he could fly and many dropped to their knees in wonder.

Molly had other ideas and, if she shielded her eyes from the bright lights, she could see the hidden wires holding the king in place. Slowly the king descended until he was standing atop the tube. Bowing theatrically before the party, King Rufus cleared his throat.

"My babies," he boomed. "You are the chosen ones. You are my destiny. The future is now and you are the future. Be brave, be strong and bring home success. The nation is depending on you. The time is now!"

With a final flourish, he waved his arms and pulled a gold lever to open the gate. The power released from the generator surged forward. It glowed fluorescent blue, and cackled and spat as it coursed into the machine. A large propeller began to rotate at the rear of the cylinder, slowly at first, then quickly gathered speed. Molly and the assembled crowd had to hold their ears as the machine roared into life. The wires wriggled like snakes as power was diverted to other areas of the machine. Lights along the banks of computers glowed brightly.

The scientists leapt into action and pulled levers, adjusted dials and pushed buttons. The large metal ring began to glow and heat up and a thin vapour appeared in its centre. The vapour began to thicken and develop into a mist, which swirled and moved around the centre of the ring. Soon the ring was completely filled with this thick mist. Shapes started to materialise in the fog, only to disappear seconds later. A bright white light shone through the mist giving a truly mystical effect.

Suddenly, lightning leapt out of the ring and struck the floor in front of the group, knocking many off their feet. This caused the scientists to leap into action and they quickly adjusted levers and knobs. The power dimmed slightly, the mist thickened a little more and a pale fluorescent blue halo appeared around the edge of the ring.

The king jumped up and down in excitement, positively shaking with anticipation. "The transporter is ready!" he screamed.

The advance party was now surrounded by guards who were linking arms to ensure that no one escaped. Slowly but surely, they squeezed the press-ganged advance party towards the planetary transporter. General Clutterberry stood in front of the imposing ring as sparks occasionally leapt out at his feet; the wizened general was unfazed and ignored them completely. In his hands, the general held a number of masks with a mouthpiece which was connected to a small pump-like contraption.

Chunky and another of the king's trusted lieutenants pushed their way through the crowd. Chunky planned to be the first moon inhabitant to set foot on the patterned planet. A moon monk rushed forward to perform spiritual incantations on the chosen two; after a quick blessing, they were declared ready. The general approached, kissed each side of Chunky's cheek and handed him a mask contraption.

"Put this on," ordered the general. "It will help you to breathe and adapt to the patterned planet's conditions."

Chunky beat his chest and roared with satisfaction. He was the one; his destiny lay seconds away. Immortality beckoned and Chunky was ready. Giving Molly a smile and a wink, he took a step onto the platform and stood before the ring. He waved to the watching crowd and then linked arms with his fellow lieutenant. The pair stood before the swirling mist with currents of electric blue streaking through the haze. No one knew what awaited the intrepid duo but Chunky was not concerned. He jumped up and down, screamed his satisfaction and then launched himself forward with his huge Moon Monkey feet.

Instantly, the two disappeared through the mist and a silent hush fell across the room. Seconds and then minutes passed and nothing happened. Basing his assumption on the lack of any body parts, the king declared the first jump a success, and promptly called the next two forward.

CHAPTER FORTY-TWO

The next two were less enthusiastic and had to be given a little encouragement, but they too eventually disappeared into the fog. The scientists studied the charts and, after a brief discussion among themselves, gave the king a big thumbs up. By their calculations, the first four invaders had landed on the patterned planet and the mission was so far a success.

Eager to get the invasion fully underway, the king ordered that the next launch be increased to three people. The chief scientist rushed forward and tried to plead with the king, but the king would have none of it and ordered his guards to push forward three more very reluctant volunteers. The three – a grizzled mwarf, a young soldier, who didn't look old enough to be in the army, and Sally Lion Head – were forced to line up side by side.

Sally stood tall and brave, her mane positively shining in the dim light, the snakes hissing and spitting. When a guard tried to push her towards the ring of mist, she swished her powerful tail and sent him sprawling against the cavern wall.

"I will cross in my own time," she shouted. "Molly, I will be waiting for you. Do not be scared. I will have your back."

With that, Sally grabbed the mask from the general, then the hands of the other two and stepped into the mist and through the ring.

Immediately, the machine began to groan and the mist within the ring began to glow bright yellow. Sparks shot out of the cylinder and the wires running around the room seemed to come alive, moving and wriggling like the snakes in Sally's hair. It was almost too much for the machine but, then, the power dimmed and faded in the huge pipes from the generators.

"More fuel!" boomed General Clutterberry.

The guards in the other room began to whip the poor, already sweating, mwarves. "You heard the man!" they screamed. "Work harder."

An extra-large tree trunk was shoved into the roaring furnace. In the intense heat it instantly burst into flames. A huge surge of energy coursed through the pipes into the next cavern and flooded into the transporter. One of the screws holding the pipes together, no longer able to take the strain, burst free of its restraint and shot across the room at incredible speed, straight towards the king.

Incredibly, using lightning reflexes that defied his age, General Clutterberry shoved the king aside. The bullet screw, that would definitely have killed the king, seared through his cheek instead. His skin exploded in a gush of blood and flesh and Rufus dropped to his knees in agony.

The cut was deep and would surely leave a scar and a lasting reminder of the day the Moon conquered the patterned planet.

Enraged and consumed with pain, he leapt to his feet and screamed at the scientists, "I want more *now*!"

One brave technician advanced to protest, but the king's temper flared. He grabbed the general's sword and rammed it straight through the unfortunate scientist, who promptly fell dead to the floor.

No one said another word in protest. A new screw was inserted and some adjustments were made to the transporter. The guards went into the huddle of the attack force. One of the guards approached Molly but at the last moment pushed her aside and grabbed the man beside her. The king now insisted that the number travelling through the machine be increased to four.

As four stood trembling at the ring of mist, the mist once again thickened to fluorescent blue and lightning streaked through the gloom. The chief scientist rapidly made adjustments and then gave the thumbs up; the machine was ready. The unhappy four resisted entering the machine, and the guards stood behind them, put the masks over their faces and, as one, shoved all four through the ring.

They disappeared instantly, but something was wrong. Funny noises were coming from the machine, almost as if it was groaning in pain. The mist turned first yellow and then red, and flames could be seen in the distance, through the mist. In one instant, the flames appeared close to bursting into the room and the next they seemed to be miles away. Suddenly, a burning image plunged into the room, glowing brightly for a few seconds as the blackened bones of a skeleton appeared to stand and then walk towards the king. A blackened skeleton arm lifted up in anger before the whole skeleton shape collapsed into a pile of smoking, smouldering ash. This was followed by a massive boom and then silence.

Everyone stared at the charred remains of one of their fellow competitors. Nobody moved, not even the king, who stood shocked and still bleeding from the wound to his cheek. Panic quickly set in and the remaining task force collectively decided that enough was enough. As one, they surged towards the exit. Molly was propelled along as they tried to make good their escape. Those in the front reached the heavy wooden door and banged on it, trying to force it open by any means. Heavy swords thudded into the door, others clubbed at it with huge axes and some just banged with their fists.

Recovering quickly, the king laughed. "There is no escape," he exclaimed. "Even if you break down the door which of course you won't, then behold!"

With a silent command, the door began to open. Molly's spirits were briefly lifted as she thought that the king had somehow come to his senses. But she couldn't have been more wrong. The door opened enough for the task force to see what lay beyond and all their life and spirit rapidly slipped away. Beyond the door was row upon row of soldiers. It was the king's entire army, in fact, armed and assembled, ready to join the invasion as soon as the task force had magnified the power at Stonehenge.

The uprising was over before it had begun. There would be no escape. All signs of resistance disappeared as the assembled group realised the only option was the transporter to the patterned planet. The guards pushed the task force back towards the ring and the doorway to another world.

The machine now stood silent and no mist swirled within the ring. It was broken. Four had been too many. Scientists and technicians scurried about, as busy as Rants. Overjoyed at preventing the break-out before it had even begun, the king was quickly becoming irate.

"Get this machine working now!" he cried, with blood streaming from his cheek and anger pulsating in his veins. He began to storm around the room, pulling at the sleeves of the scientists, pushing them and prodding them, cajoling them into action.

Time passed slowly as screws were tightened, cables checked and replaced, tubes repaired and machines recalibrated. More moontree logs, collected and stored over many years, were transported down from the surface, ready to fuel the giant furnace.

Finally, the chief scientist approached the king. "Sire, I believe we are ready. But I must advise caution. We cannot overload the device again. It will not take it!"

King Rufus fumed, swore obscenities but, in the end, had to agree; even the king could see that the invasion was doomed without the space-travelling machine. Gradually, he calmed down. "Two it is then and I want to choose. You," he shouted, pointing to Bobbin Good. "Yes, young man. Your time is up."

Guards made a grab for Bobbin and made him stand at the ring.

"Who's next?" mused the king, enjoying his power and taking his time. "A female, I feel, to go along with the young man. Yes, I know," said the king. "You there!"

All eyes turned to where he pointed. Molly looked behind her to see who everyone was looking at. Shocked, she realised that there was, in fact, no one behind her and all eyes were on her. Her knees went weak and she was overcome with despair. Before she had time to react or accept the king's choice, she was roughly grabbed and hoisted alongside Bobbin.

"Yes!" cried the king, clearly happy with his choice. "A perfect match. Go forth my heroes and make the Moon proud."

Molly felt anything but a hero. She was shaking and, despite trying hard not to, tears rolled down her cheeks.

"Be brave," whispered Bobbin, who gently took hold of Molly's hand. "You are not alone and Carnaverous says 'Hello'."

Surprised, Molly looked into the young man's face and could see only braveness and kindness. Bobbin Good stood tall and proud and a little of his resilience began to rub off on Molly.

Taking deep breaths, she began to calm herself and take control. "I am Molly of the Fogey's. I am champion crater walker of the entire Moon. I can do this." She repeated this to herself over and over. As she did, she began to straighten her back, stand taller and puff out her chest. Which was lucky, because the machine was ready.

Molly and Bobbin stood before the ring. Dense fog filled and swirled around the centre; nothing could be seen beyond. Neon blue streaks of energy shot across the fog, producing stunning shapes and patterns.

Still holding hands and without being forced, they fixed the masks on their faces and the intrepid duo stepped through the ring and into the unknown.

Molly instantly felt a rush. Her fingernails and toenails began to quiver and stretch, as if someone was tugging at them with a set of blacksmith's tongs. The pain moved to her toes and fingers; someone was trying to pull them off. The sensation moved to her feet and hands as each body part was stretched and tugged. The pain was unbearable, but worse was to come. Molly could feel her eyes beginning to bulge, as if someone was trying to pluck her eyes out. Teeth followed eyes, as each tooth felt as if it was being pulled out. Molly tried to scream, but she no longer had a tongue or a mouth.

That was the last thing she remembered before she passed out.

CHAPTER FORTY-THREE

Mank and Ratabat were having their own adventures. Mank missed Molly badly and was determined to find her. Ratabat was perched on the cat's back and they looked a very odd combination, like a miniature horse and cloaked rider. For once, being small was to their advantage. The intrepid duo had crept through the castle and followed the army through the underground caverns. Easily evading capture and often darting between soldiers' legs, the pair were hiding in a dark crevice watching all of the events unfold. Mank's claws dug deep into the rock. He hissed and spat as he watched Molly disappear. Ratabat's claws were out too. As it hopped up and down, the claws unintentionally dug into Mank, making the cat even angrier. Suddenly and with a power that defied Mank's appearance, he charged towards the contraption and the ring of mist. Ratabat clung on for dear life and rode the cat like a professional rodeo rider. Cat and bat bounded towards the mist.

Screeching as he went, Mank grabbed a mask and breathing pump in his mouth from the stunned general, and took a huge leap straight into the mist and through the centre of the ring. Those who saw this could only watch on in disbelief. What in the name of the moon gods had they just seen? To many, it looked like a miniature version of the grim reaper riding a miniature horse of the Apocalypse. They dropped to their knees in horror, convinced that the image was an ill omen for the future.

Even the king was stunned. He performed a swift incantation of protection and quickly crossed his chest.

This, however, was short-lived and even as the trailing cat hairs drifted slowly to the ground, the king was back in control. Shouting and demanding once again, King Rufus wanted the next two volunteers lined up.

CHAPTER FORTY-FOUR

Molly was quickly reassembling within the circle of stone monoliths. Her feet were firmly planted on the ground, although at the moment, she couldn't feel the lush, damp, chilled, slippery grass through her toes. Reforming from her feet up, her legs started to take shape, followed by her body and arms. As her head began to form, something very unexpected occurred. One eye popped into her head, quickly followed by the other, but they appeared where her mouth should have been. There was no stopping the process and, before she knew what was happening, Molly's mouth appeared in her forehead.

Bobbin Good, who was lucky enough to have reformed correctly, tried hard to stifle a laugh. Molly's head was correctly positioned on her young shoulders but her nose was missing and her face was upside down. Next, Molly's nose appeared where her ear should be. What a disaster.

Sally Lion Head rushed up to Molly and quickly squeezed her with all her strength.

Like popping candy, the sudden surge of pressure

caused Molly's features to rearrange around her head. Her nose fell into place but her eyes continued to roll around, before coming to rest. One eye was perfect but the other was positioned halfway down her cheek. Sally gave Molly a final big squeeze and, with a swift plop, her eye popped back into place.

At last, Molly was complete, although she was feeling decidedly weird. She dropped to her knees in the damp grass and quickly retrieved the mask which had fallen off on reassembly. Molly was struggling to breathe; the air felt heavy, as if she was chewing on moon mud. However, once Molly had the mask and breather on her face, she began to feel a little better.

It still took several minutes for Molly to come to her senses. At first, she became aware of a tremendous weight on her shoulders almost pushing her down; others in the group were moving very slowly, almost in slow motion. Next, Molly became aware of the strange sensation of the sweet-smelling, cool slippery feel of fresh grass, something that only the king's favourites had experienced in his special garden. Molly's mind strayed back to that time in the mystical garden and the ramblings of the king as he hatched his dastardly plans.

Now her correctly positioned eyes grew wide in wonder. The patterned planet was amazing. Bright lights flashed in the distance followed by strange rumbling noises. Molly dropped her head in the grass and filled her senses with the exquisite experience. The sweet smell was intoxicating; the strange little flowers dotted around the grass were beautiful.

The place was out of this world. When Molly finally looked up, her wonderment only grew. Huge great slabs of rock rose out of the ground, standing tall and proud, massive and majestic.

She was in awe of the amazing monoliths spread over a large area of ground that seemed to from a rough circle, with a small inner horseshoe that completed the stunning scene.

Molly's joy was short-lived. Chunky roughly tugged her to her feet.

"They're only stones," he growled. "You have a job to do."

Chunky, however, seemed to have lost some of his usual self-assurance and confidence. He was moving ever so slow; his huge Moon Monkey feet were proving a hindrance rather than a help in this strange place.

Now would have been the perfect time to start a revolt but, at that very moment, General Clutterberry appeared next to Chunky and took control of the proceedings, calming things down and barking orders at the frightened landing party. The old general took all of the new experiences in his stride and just shrugged them off.

Moving in slow motion the general grabbed Molly hard and started shaking her by the shoulders. He urged her on. "C'mon, girl. You know the plan. So, get to it."

Turning to Chunky, the general treated the huge Moon Monkey just as gruffly. "Pull yourself together, man. You are the king's representative here. Give the girl her tools," he bellowed.

The general's swift remarks worked wonders on

Chunky who immediately reverted to his old horrible self. Rather reluctantly and with menace on his mind, Chunky roughly handed Molly her equipment which he had taken from her before he departed for the patterned planet.

Chunky then threw a large satchel a little too hard at Molly, who dropped the contents all over the ground, earning Chunky a clip around the ear from the general. "Careful, you buffoon. That is delicate equipment that you are just throwing around!"

By now, Chunky was absolutely seething and, in his eyes, all this was Molly's fault. He was determined to exact his revenge. He had a plan and Molly was not going to return home a hero.

CHAPTER FORTY-FIVE

Molly scrabbled around on her knees collecting up the strange little machines and replacing them back in the satchel. The crater rope was a basic standard crater rope like many found on the Moon, although this one had a three-pronged sharp hook attached to one end. Molly walked to the nearest stone and coiled the rope at her feet. Slowly approaching the large stone, she reached out and touched the cold, hard rock face. Ancient and old, Molly could feel the power and mystery resonate through the stone. The stones were almost humming and, to Molly, it seemed that they were talking to her in an archaic language; possibly they were trying to get a message to her. But she was frustrated. She simply couldn't understand.

Chunky suddenly pulled her back roughly. "Get on with it, peasant, and remember I am watching you closely," he spat in her face.

Molly's patience finally broke. Feeling utterly alone, intensely angry and frightened, she was about to fly into a rage and to hell with the consequences. But Sally Lion Head was close by and she immediately stepped in between the two before things got ugly.

With her back to Chunky, Sally gently held Molly's head in her hands. "Calm down," Sally whispered. "We are with you. Look for the sign. You will know."

"Enough," boomed the general. "We are running out of time. Get on with it now. The army is waiting."

Molly had no choice but to obey. Giving Sally Lion Head a quick hug, she bent down and picked up the crater rope. Slowly at first, she began to swing the hooked rope, which felt much heavier than usual but gradually it picked up speed. The rope slid through her hands, the friction burning her fingers. The arc of the swing grew and grew, getting quicker and quicker.

Swiftly the rope shot outwards, travelling at immense speed, the hook travelling towards the top of the huge slab of ancient stone. Flying high into the night sky, the grappling hook hit the top of the giant slab and slid across the damp moss-covered surface before it took hold. Molly gave a tug and the rope appeared secure.

"You try first," ordered the general. "I don't want the contents of the satchel damaged."

The general's years of experience once again held him in good stead. As soon as Molly started to climb the rope, the grip of the hook gave way. The hook sailed past Molly, narrowly missing her left shoulder, and soon she went tumbling after it. She landed with an embarrassing thump on her behind and the watching crowd couldn't help but break into muffled laughter.

General Clutterberry was not amused. He ordered silence and then roughly pulled Molly up and told her in no uncertain terms to get on with things.

Dusting herself down and glowing with embarrassment, she repeated the actions of before. She was determined not to fail this time and when the hook once again left her hand, it was with greater intensity and purpose. The hook and rope flew true and clean, landing exactly where Molly had aimed; there would be no mistake this time. The hook's grip was secure and Molly, wasting no time, shimmied up the dangling rope.

The hardest part was dragging herself over the edge and onto the top of the stone but once there, she stood tall and, despite her concerns, raised her arms to the sky in short-lived triumph. The Moon hovered large in the dark sky and beamed back at her, shiny and bright. She could only look in awe at her home and briefly wondered what her friends were doing right now and if they were worried about her. Next, it was Sally Lion Head's turn, with two huge lengths of wire, one red and one black; both wrapped around her shoulder and waist, she approached the base. The wire was heavy but with the help of Molly, Sally was soon also on top of the first giant monolith.

Sally and Molly hugged and huddled together on top of the stone. The respite was short-lived, as a small stone painfully hit Molly in the midriff. It was Chunky, demanding that she pull the rest of the rope up, with the satchel and its mysterious contents attached to the end. Gently, Molly pulled the rope up the side of the huge stone and safely placed the bag down beside here before gingerly opening the zip.

Carefully, she lifted the first of the small machines out. It was dark, shiny and cube-shaped, and a mist similar to the one that Molly had stepped through earlier swirled deep within it. On the top were two gold connectors and a switch. Sally Lion Head took the end of each wire, that was currently wrapped around her, and handed them to Molly. She now had two wires, one red and one black, one for each connector. It was Molly's job to wrap the wire around the gold connector and, using her crater walking skills, link the stones by the wires and connectors. She quickly secured the cube to the first stone and then completed her next task of wrapping the wires around the gold connectors.

The general, who was watching closely, barked at her, "Flick the switch, girl."

With the king's landing party all watching expectantly, Molly had no choice but to do as she was told. Where was her help? Where was Carnaverous? What was the plan? Time was running out. How, for moon's sake, was she going to stop this madness? She had no idea.

The cube began to hum and glow in the eerie morning half-light, almost as if it were alive. The mist within danced and swirled and for a second Molly thought that she saw the king, marshalling his forces back on the Moon.

"Good girl," urged the general. "Now get on with it."

CHAPTER FORTY-SIX

Picking up the grappling hook, Molly once again spun the rope faster and faster. This time she shot the rope out sideways, straight and true, towards the next giant stone, which stood a short distance away. The hook gripped straight away. Molly pulled the rope tight and secured the other end to the surface of the rock upon which she was standing. Once the rope was taut, Molly picked up the satchel and placed it on her back. She then confidently hopped onto the rope.

Despite the darkness, the crossing should have been child's play to Molly and she could have done it with her eyes closed. However, Molly was feeling a little weird and light-headed, the rope felt heavy and Molly felt as if she was going to faint. Just as Molly's legs began to buckle and she was sure she was going to fall, Sally Lion Head was immediately there by her side. Promptly holding Molly up, Sally told her to take some deep breaths into the mask and suck in moon-processed air through the pump.

The conditions on the patterned planet were having

a strange effect on members of the landing party including Molly. General Clutterberry, growing increasingly impatient, shouted at the pair to get a chuffing move on. Sally shouted back and as the pair argued Molly began to recover and felt a bit better. Why couldn't they breathe properly? Molly wondered. But not for long as Chunky had launched another stone at her and the stones were getting bigger. Molly was forced to try again; with the satchel on her back she gingerly crossed the rope to the second stone. Once Molly was secure, Sally Lion Head, with the two wires trailing behind her, also crossed the second rope.

Soon, both were on the second stone. Molly crouched down, took the satchel from her back and removed the next cube. As before, she fixed the two wires to the gold connectors. She paused for a while then, hoping beyond hope for help. When none was forthcoming, she flicked the switch. The cube leapt into life, brighter than the first. The power was already growing, and electricity crackled and spat from the cube, and mist swirled and seemed to ooze from it. Molly could almost run her hand through it. This time she could clearly see the king, acting his normal bossy self and pushing the scientists about. The larger portal was beginning to open.

Molly was now getting ready to move onto the next stone. The task was tiring and a little strange with the conditions and Molly was now using this to her advantage; she was taking every opportunity to delay the inevitable. Deliberately swaying on the rope, she stumbled and hesitated whenever she could. Chunky, however, was getting wise to her tricks and every time he thought she was going particularly slowly, a spear flew close to her rear, just to speed her up a bit.

Despite trying her best to delay proceedings, Molly was already halfway around the circle with Sally at her side. Half of the cubes were now set up and Molly was sure that the hum that they were producing would surely bring the locals out to investigate. However, apart from some strange moving lights that sped along in different directions, the landing party had so far not been disturbed.

Molly was becoming increasingly concerned as streaks of lightning were now regularly shooting from cube to cube, sometimes linking up and growing white-hot for several seconds. Someone was sure to come and investigate the noise and lights and Molly was very worried. She didn't want to complete the circle and, yet, the slower she was, the greater the risk of discovery. She didn't know what to do. She had never felt so alone and disaster lurked at every turn.

It was then that Sally Lion Head grabbed her hand and seemed to nod her great fluffy mane in encouragement, as if willing her on. Molly took this as a sign that she must continue, push on and pray that a miracle would happen.

Molly continued on and every time she linked another cube, the power grew. Intense beams of light streaked from cube to cube. Laser-like in appearance, the beams of light criss-crossed the interior of the circle, and a mist started to form in the centre of the stones. The mist, which had started small, was now swirling and lapping at the feet of the assembled task force. There was only one stone remaining and the circle would be complete; it looked as if no help was coming. The king's plan was going to succeed. War was about to begin.

With a heavy heart, Molly switched the next cube on and now prepared to step once more onto the first stone, to complete the circle, and that would be it. Thousands of the king's finest men would soon be charging through the portal. Molly again tried to delay the inevitable, deliberately failing to hook the final stone with her rope. She tried to claim that the stone was too far away and she couldn't reach it.

Knowing that Bobbin Good was Molly's ally, Chunky grabbed him and held a sharp knife to his neck. "It had better reach and soon," he shouted. "Or your friend's blood will be the first moon blood spilt on the patterned planet."

Molly had no choice. For the final time, she spun her rope. The rope shot out into the dawn light. This time the hook stretched across the gap with ease, clanked heavily onto the stone, the very stone where she began her task, and gripped solid. Molly tightened the rope; it was ready and she was ready. It was time to make the final crossing. She had run out of excuses and she couldn't be responsible for Bobbin's death. Reluctantly, she jumped onto the rope, which swayed gently. She adjusted her balance and began to cross.

Slowly, she inched across the rope, but the last stone approached far too quickly for Molly's liking. It wasn't long before she was atop the stone. She could feel the ancient giant's power beneath her bare feet. Sally was right behind her and removed the two ends of the wires from her body and handed them to Molly to place them onto the connectors. The circle would now be complete.

Molly prayed for help. "Come on, Carnaverous. Where are you?" she urged, but only silence replied. The game was up.

She continued with her task, pulling the red wire and the black wire close to the connectors. It was then that something completely unexpected occurred. Out of the blue and just as she was about to connect the red wire, Molly noticed a shift in her surroundings. Dumbfounded, she could only stop and stare at what was happening.

The air around Molly seemed to draw in on itself. She could feel the pressure pulling on her as the mist from the cubes was sucked towards the anomaly. Gradually, a ghostly form began to take shape. The apparition seemed to hover in and out of existence, desperately trying to take hold, drawing on all the power from the surrounding area. For an instant, the form grew in strength and appeared more solid. Molly's jaw dropped. Relief surged through her veins and she couldn't quite believe it. It was Carnaverous the Great. He had answered her prayers. He had not let her down and help had finally arrived.

Carnaverous, however, was beginning to fade away again, the energy draining from him.

"No," cried Molly and she grabbed his ghostly hand and pulled.

It was just what he required. Using some of Molly's nervous energy, he sucked more life into himself.

Carnaverous now looked more solid and more complete. He smiled at Molly and mouthed, "Sorry I am so late. The timing is crucial and we don't have long."

With this, he pushed Molly away rather roughly, grabbed the two wires and quickly held the red and the black to each other. The result was instantaneous, causing a massive short circuit to the system.

Carnaverous grew bright white and Molly could feel heat radiating from his ghost-like figure. Suddenly, the ghostly face cracked completely open, the head split in half, and each side flopped in the cool air. What followed next was truly shocking. The air fizzled and crackled. One moment, Carnaverous was smiling at Molly, and the next he had completely exploded into a thousand pieces. A sonic boom followed, so loud that the local inhabitants were still talking about the mysterious goings-on years later.

The blast sent Molly and Sally flying from the top of the stone. Molly landed heavily on the ground. Badly winded, she could only lie there. She knew she would be badly bruised and very sore, but she didn't think she had broken anything. There was no trace of Carnaverous.

The stone circle fell silent, and no one could quite comprehend what had just occurred.

CHAPTER FORTY-SEVEN

Chunky was the first to recover and he was in a right rage. Grabbing an axe from the nearest warrior, he charged towards Molly. "What have you done, you idiot?" he snarled. "You'll pay for this with your life."

Molly was in no position to move and could only curl up to try to protect herself.

Suddenly, out of the darkness swept Ratabat, straight into Chunky's face. The little bat squawked and flapped, its small talons scratching at the Moon Monkey's eyes. Chunky, temporarily blinded, stopped his pursuit of Molly and staggered around clutching at his face. Luckily for Molly, Mank was next on the scene; the weight of the two friends was considerably less than that of the heavily armed task force. Because of that, they had been transported to a completely different place, and had arrived at the mayhem at the stone circle just in time.

Mank rushed between Chunky's legs. In a panic and unable to see, the unfortunate Moon Monkey, who was still running, tripped and crashed to the ground, bashing his head on a rock as he landed. He lay on the ground, dazed and confused, no longer a threat. Mank and Ratabat rushed to Molly's side.

The danger, however, had only increased. General Clutterberry, recovering from the shock of the doomed mission, was already rallying his troops. He wanted Molly's head on a plate.

The men advanced on the three friends and were nearly upon them when, as one, they stopped abruptly. All heads looked up and Molly slowly followed. High in the sky a glowing hole appeared like a large eye. Burning bright orange around the edges and turquoise in the centre, it glittered in the night sky. For what seemed an eternity, but was in fact mere minutes, the monstrous eye seemed to glare at the landing party. Then, it began to rotate. Slowly at first, but then quickly gathering speed, the eye spun and spun. A low rumble began to growl and the wind picked up. Molly and the assembled army were pushed and pulled about by the growing tempest. Growing in strength, the ferocious spinning eye began to emit a spiralling plume of air; a deadly tornado was forming, dragging in the surrounding air as it rapidly gained power.

Carnaverous's actions had triggered a powerful chain reaction. As quick as...well...lightning, a bolt shot from the eye and struck one of the cubes, obliterating it. This was followed by a large crack of thunder that hurt Molly's eardrums.

Then the heavens opened. This was a new experience for the moon dwellers, as they had never seen rain before.

They were soon drenched to the skin, cold and frightened. Molly quite liked the sensation of the cold wet drops punching her skin.

The spinning column of air was now colossal. It stretched from the spinning eye towards the ground. Wind shrieked through the stones, which seemed to groan under the strain. A small tree branch smashed into Molly, knocking the breath out of her. Her skin prickled with the cold and her fingers were numb from clinging to the sodden earth.

The rain hurt Molly's eyes, but as she looked through the darkening gloom, she could see Mank grimly holding onto Ratabat, trying his best to hold onto the bat with his padded paws only and just managing not to use his claws. Molly's friends were in very real danger of being sucked away. She had to save them. She slowly inched her way towards the pair. Lightning struck the ground between them, the grass turned black and scorched; the smell of burning ozone made Molly's nose tickle and her eyes sting.

Clinging to the ground with all her strength and using her hands and feet to grip at anything she could, Molly closed the gap between them. The raging tempest whistled through her ears, as she reached out and grabbed her friends. Pulling them close and clutching them tightly to her chest, Molly was temporarily relieved. This action, however, seemed to enrage the storm even more. Unbelievably, the wind grew in strength, the rain lashed at Molly, and heavy cold lumps of ice struck her hard.

Suddenly, the twister touched the ground and then all hell broke loose. It picked up a tree as if it was a small stick, which smashed into one of the giant stones. With a huge thunderous bang, the tree broke like tinder, while another smashed to the ground close to Molly. A small mwarf was powerfully knocked off his feet and, before he could regain his footing, was swept up into the towering, circling tunnel of wind. Molly watched as the unfortunate soul went round and round, getting closer and closer to the giant eye in the sky. With a flourish of arms and legs, he disappeared.

The twister swept across the inner stone circle, hoovering up anything and anyone in its deadly path. General Clutterberry decided to make a run for it. Fleeing for his life, the old man managed just a few yards. The spiralling air seemed to sense his movement, changed course and hunted him down. Moments later, like an invisible hand, it lifted the unfortunate general by the ankles. He hovered for some seconds, dangling upside down in the air, and then, whoosh; round and round, up and up, the general disappeared skywards towards the eye. The spinning torrent of air was warming to its task, gaining power with every moon inhabitant that it sucked inside.

Howling in anger, the tempest sensed every movement; no one could outrun it. One clever Samhain Mage waited for the tornado to tear across the stone circle in the opposite direction and then decided to magically run for it, moving at a speed that no man could naturally achieve. The Mage very nearly escaped, until a massive lightning bolt shot from the eye, instantly striking and obliterating the Mage.

Sally Lion Head was next to disappear, her fluffy mane the last part of her to be seen swirling up the column of wind. Only a few of the moon raiders now remained. Molly crawled under the shattered tree and stayed stock still. She was covered by flying debris, tree, leaves and twigs completely concealing her, Ratabat and Mank, as the tornado continued to hoover all around her. Chunky had used Molly's crater rope to secure himself to one of the stones and had so far evaded the carnage that was happening all around.

Impossibly, the storm grew in intensity. A huge surge of wind swirled, danced and began to take on the shape of a huge Moon Monkey three times the size of Chunky. Intensely angry, this wind monster advanced on Chunky; with each step, the massive wind monkey left a deep indentation on the ground. Even the huge stone that Chunky was secured to seemed to buckle under the strain. He stood no chance. Huge hands of pure wind and power tore at the ropes that secured him. The rope resisted for seconds but was soon in shreds.

Chunky came out fighting, trying his best to kick and punch at the wind monster. But each blow simply disappeared into fresh air. The wind seemed to mock him, tugging and pulling at him. It grabbed at his legs, causing Chunky to land heavily on his bum. Next, it pulled roughly on his hair, causing Chunky to howl in pain. Quickly growing bored with this game, the wind monster opened its huge jaws, revealing dangerously sharp teeth and a dark cavernous abyss. It inhaled sharply, sweeping Chunky off his feet and into the air like a feather. The wind monster closed its mouth and Chunky instantly disappeared.

With its hunger satisfied, the wind monster burst into a thousand small tornadoes that tore across the stone circle. The much larger tornado chased after them and swept them up, like a mother collecting her babies.

The wind dropped and the power of the eye was beginning to wane. The baby tornadoes had all been collected and all of the moon invaders had been sucked up through the eye.

CHAPTER FORTY-EIGHT

All of the moon invaders, that is, apart from Molly and her two friends who remained concealed under the broken tree. The eye and the wind monster had missed them and the wind funnel was now only occasionally touching the ground. From her hiding place, Molly held her breath and watched as the tornado diminished in size, as it disappeared upwards towards the hovering eye in the sky. Molly had survived. But now what? She was stranded on the patterned planet.

Unfortunately, the eye still had plans for Molly. It suddenly grew a brilliant white, and lightning shot out all around its edges. The weakening tornado grew in power again. Hailstones the size of Chunky's fist rained down on the stone circle and the tree protecting Molly was smashed to bits. Then, two burning balls of white-hot lightning blasted to smithereens what remained of the tree, leaving Molly completely exposed.

Molly, Mank and Ratabat shook with fear. The twister moved back towards the ground with immense speed, growing ever closer to the three friends.

Fear not, Molly, exclaimed a voice in Molly's head.

It sounded like Carnaverous, but she thought that was impossible; she had seen the great man destroyed with her own eyes. The voice, however, sounded friendly and instantly Molly felt calmer and she relaxed.

Two strong hands seemed to form within the powerful twister, gently lifting Molly and her friends into the air. However, once caught in the gushing, howling tempest, they began to spin. Round and round, faster and faster, Molly was twisted and turned, her muscles felt as if they were being pulled apart, and she began to feel sick and dizzy. Bright lights flashed in her mind; strange images appeared and disappeared, including one that showed Molly as a baby in a crib with a stern-looking king peering in at her.

Then she blacked out.

CHAPTER FORTY-NINE

Molly's tale ends where it began. The first thing she became aware of as she regained consciousness was a big gnarly hand swinging her by the hair and letting go.

Battered and crumpled, Molly landed at the feet of a very angry King Rufus. The tornado had sucked Molly and her friends through its eye and returned them home. But they did not receive a very warm welcome.

The king was incandescent with rage. He landed a brutal kick straight into Molly's ribs, winding her and causing indescribable pain. She curled into a ball and cried. The king was about to land another powerful blow when General Clutterberry, himself injured and battered, stepped in between the king and Molly.

"Sire," said the general, "people are watching. You cannot kill a defenceless girl. It will end in revolt. Calm yourself now."

With these wise words from the general, the king turned to see the recently returned landing party all staring at him. Anger simmered behind many of the watching eyes.

Breathing deeply to try to control his anger, the king recognised the truth in the general's words and stepped back from his onslaught. He ordered a guard to lift Molly up by the shoulders; he couldn't resist one final insult. He walked up and spat in Molly's face. Barely conscious, she was incapable of reacting.

"Search her and then throw her into the dungeon and let her rot!" screamed the king. "Oh, and throw that foul-smelling cat and disgusting rat with wings in with her!"

Filthy hands searched Molly roughly. She tried to protest but the guards were too strong and Molly too weak. They removed all that Molly had left, even her shoes, which was very bad as these contained the Nitsplitter, thus leaving Molly defenceless.

She was dragged to the grimmest, filthiest, blackest dungeon in the castle and thrown in, landing with a thump on the cold damp floor. The guards laughed as one of them turned the big key in the lock and they walked back up the dark corridor.

Molly was left in darkness, half alive and with Mank and Ratabat at her side. The only thing the guards had missed was the small pebble that the Rant had given her the day she fell into the crater.

Cold and scared, Molly rubbed it for comfort and cried herself to sleep.

To Be Continued…